PERSONAL
WARS

To Dolly

PERSONAL WARS

Thank you

Enjoy

Dick Barry

RICHARD V. BARRY

Winterlight Books
Shelbyville, KY USA

Personal Wars
by Richard V. Barry

Copyright © 2010 Richard V. Barry
ALL RIGHTS RESERVED

First Printing – November 2010
ISBN: 978-1-60047-503-0

NO PART OF THIS BOOK MAY BE REPRODUCED IN ANY FORM, BY PHOTOCOPYING OR BY ANY ELECTRONIC OR MECHANICAL MEANS, INCLUDING INFORMATION STORAGE OR RETRIEVAL SYSTEMS, WITHOUT PERMISSION IN WRITING FROM THE COPYRIGHT OWNER/AUTHOR

Printed in the U.S.A.

TO

GAYLE AND STEPHEN, SERENA AND RUSSELL

*And the mysterious, blessed alchemy that
turns friends into family–*

A FRIEND MAY WELL BE RECKONED THE MASTERPIECE OF NATURE.
Ralph Waldo Emerson

WAR IS CRUEL AND YOU CANNOT REFINE IT.
William Tecumseh Sherman

OLDER MEN DECLARE WAR. BUT IT IS YOUTH THAT MUST FIGHT AND DIE. AND IT IS YOUTH WHO MUST INHERIT THE TRIBULATIONS, THE SORROW... OF WAR.
Herbert Hoover

AS LONG AS THERE ARE SOVERIGN NATIONS POSSESSING GREAT POWER, WAR IS INEVITABLE.
Albert Einstein

THE SWORD WITHIN THE SCABBARD KEEP, AND LET MANKIND AGREE.
John Dryden

Table of Contents

INTRODUCTION	1
MISSING THE MARK	4
URGENT LOVE	13
ANY PLACE LIKE THIS	19
FILTERED TRUTHS	38
REALITY CHECK	54
THE HOME FRONT	77
HANDS	92
RUTH AND NAOMI	103
DEEP WATERS	116
APRIL UPDATES	121
TOO GOOD TO BE TRUE	144
ALBERT RESURGENT	155
PARTING SHOTS	165
SUPPERTIME	179
THE DEFINING MOMENT	191
A MATTER OF CHOICE	201
THE DEAD OF NIGHT	212

Introduction

From time immemorial man has used war to settle disputes, channel aggression, satisfy ambitions, support religious intolerance and exterminate enemies. Infrequently have wars been waged purely in defense of liberty or to cast off tyranny, as exemplified by Haiti with the French and The United States with the British. Throughout our long march up from the slimy ooze to our race to the stars, we have evolved, developed and flourished; yet, war remains our constant, insidious companion, so innately a part of our genetic code, it seems, that we cannot forsake it or find a better, healthier outlet for the darker forces of our nature. Instead, we rationalize it, using words like justice, honor, glory and retribution. At times we have claimed to fight wars to achieve a lasting peace, but that lofty goal eludes us and back to the battlefields we march.

Especially in our modern era, it is not just the combatants who engage in war and become its casualties; vast civilian populations also become potential victims when swept up in the devastating maelstrom of modern armaments and widespread targets. London,

Dresden, Hiroshima and Baghdad come immediately to mind. Over fifty million people lost their lives in World War II—a staggering statistic—and the First World War was viewed as the war to end all wars, so cataclysmic was its effect on the human psyche. Still, wars large and small have been waged in every corner of the globe since those epical mass destructions. In this area alone we can make no headway and seem doomed to repeat the mistakes of all previous generations. Science is used as much to create instruments of man's annihilation as it is to improve man's existence.

As a writer, I ponder these troubling issues and find no satisfactory answers, but the subject of war haunts me. Our country is currently engaged in two wars that seem interminable and have been pushed to the sidelines, sporadically arresting our attention only by news bulletins on television or in print. One percent of our citizenry is fighting, suffering and dying in these wars, while the rest of us go about our daily lives, mostly unmindful of their sacrifice and the sacrifice of their loved ones—an affront, I believe, to the underlying concepts of a noble democracy.

In these stories I'm interested in conveying the personal effects of war on individual soldiers and the civilians who celebrate, love, comfort and mourn them. The ferocious intensity of actual warfare and its starkly dehumanizing nature is a larger canvas only peripherally depicted as background to the center of each story: "the human heart in conflict with itself."[*]

Dealing with any aspect of war, as it affects both the participants and the witnesses, is potentially a bleak subject, but small, personal triumphs can emerge through courage, love and resilience. Heroism can be an unrecognized and unsung quality played out in the daily lives of ordinary people confronted with extraordinary challenges. Without mitigating the personal costs, war also gives testament to man's indomitable spirit.

---

[*] William Faulkner, Nobel Prize Acceptance Speech

Missing The Mark

It's a beautiful spring morning in Washington. The cherry blossoms are dazzling the tourists along the Tidal Basin and buds are visible everywhere I look. Small new leaves, almost transparent in their light green coatings, are peeping out from trees, reminding me that this is a season of renewal, a new cycle of life, a time of promise and hope. The air is crisp, not yet warmed by the early morning sun, and traffic is already heavy on all the roads intersecting the corridors of power as the government's engine roars to life for another day.

I remind myself that I am here for one purpose only, for which I left my home in Baltimore before the sun was up and drove directly to this spot in Washington. I'm compulsive about this and do it every year on Adam's birthday. I can't explain why: out of frustration or anger or longing or despair. It's all jumbled in my head, and I just know that I have to come to the Vietnam Memorial to honor my son because his country did not.

My wife Cathy seems to understand. She knows that I have to do this alone. She packs a lunch for me the night before and says

"Have a safe trip," before kissing me goodnight. I don't visit the World War II Memorial because that was my war. I lived it and survived it and don't want to be reminded of the carnage I saw, the buddies I lost and the paralyzing fear I experienced on islands in the South Pacific. Their names I had never heard before and could hardly pronounce until I was on those beachheads under a shower of bullets, crawling over dead and mangled bodies and around craters kissed by enemy shells, mindlessly inching forward, hating everything—a zombie-like killing machine.

By the time it was over for me and I came back to the States, the hatred was so deep inside me, like a cancer, and it took a long time for me to work it out. Many nights I'd be back on those beachheads, praying to stay alive, shooting at anything that moved in front of me, sometimes puking my guts out as I inched forward on my belly, sometimes losing control of my bowels. And always sweating heavily no matter what the temperature, seeing things hazily through sweat-drenched eyes and screaming a long litany of curse words at the top of my lungs in defiance of the enemy, of the odds against me, of God and my fate, only to wake in the fiercely wrapped arms of Cathy and return to consciousness with the hum of the soothing sounds she made in my ear. No, that's not a fucking chapter of my life I want to revisit.

We Carver men always seem to be strategically placed for each generation's war. My grandfather made it into the Spanish American War; my father, a veteran of World War I, who I know was in the thick of things and had his lungs damaged from mustard gas and came back and started his family. I never heard any war stories directly from him because he died when I was seven. I have a picture of him in uniform before going overseas, looking juvenile, innocent and proud, and a manila envelope with several of his medals that I've always been meaning to mount in a display frame with his picture but have never gotten around to it. What he experienced in that war—the war to end all wars was how the world, with blind optimism, styled it—can only be guessed by comparing his early army picture with the snapshots of him with me on my seventh birthday: the prematurely gray hair, the hard, steady gaze of his eyes and the deep creases tracing his brow and circling his mouth that belie his age—early thirties. Beneath his half-closed lids I see a haunted look in my father's eyes that speaks confidentially to me of imaginable horrors indelibly imprinted on his inner core and of recurrent pain borne with silent fortitude. Cathy saw a great resemblance between my father and me after I came back from my war, especially, she said, around the eyes. Maybe haunted men all share a common look.

At least for my father and me, we knew that any sacrifice we were called to make was in defending freedom against aggressors who would have enslaved us. We weren't just fighting for our lives; we were fighting to protect our loved ones and everything we believed in.

Then along came Adam, my first and only son after three girls, a happy, carefree and careless kid from the time he was a baby to his twentieth year when, having flunked out of college, he was drafted for Vietnam. At first, like many kids, he saw it as an adventure, a lark, and was excited to be trained as a helicopter pilot. He ran night missions along the Ho Chi Min Trail and, as he said in his infrequent letters, shooting at everything. Sometimes his letters would be dark and somber and he'd confess to not knowing why the hell he was in that hot, stinking hellhole. Other letters would be stream of consciousness with disconnected thoughts that we couldn't make sense of.

Adam made it though his tour of duty, surviving two helicopter crashes unscathed, and he came home, but the man inhabiting my son's body was an imposter, a stranger: nervous, restless, volatile, withdrawn, and furtive. Helplessly, we watched his life spiral out of control: job hopping and two short marriages and two children whom he didn't seem to care about, and endless brawls, car wrecks, arrests and short jail terms, and fruitless rehabilitation programs for drug and alcohol addiction.

"Dad, I just can't seem to get my life together," he confessed to me before he left Baltimore and moved to Texas, then Nevada and finally California where he worked as a helicopter pilot doing aerial shots for movies. Different locations, more wives and two more kids, an occasional Christmas card or phone call on his mother's birthday, his voice flushed with a heightened enthusiasm that told us his addictions were still not in control.

Cathy and I went to see him as a surprise for his thirty-fifth birthday. He had always discouraged visits and we finally realized why. We found him living in a squalid, cramped apartment in Los

Angeles—the basement of a decrepit three-family house—with a young woman named Robin who was cheerfully sweet and nursing a five-month-old baby named Pearl.

Adam was not happy to see us and I couldn't blame him. He looked at least fifteen years older than his actual age and was drinking heavily. Robin told us that he had been fired from his last movie job and hadn't worked in six months. I found a chance to be alone with him and, stupidly, vented my anger and frustration, ordering him to shape up, be a man and take responsibility for his life. He listened to my fatherly tirade and when I was finished, he started to laugh and his laughter grew into almost hysterical convulsions. Then he looked directly at me and said, "Get the fuck out of my life and leave me alone."

I gave Robin a large check for herself and the baby and Cathy and I flew home the next morning. Robin called about two months later to say that Adam had disappeared over a month ago and to ask if we knew where he was. We didn't. We never heard from Adam again. We appealed to veterans' groups and eventually hired private investigators. Nothing. My son had vanished, but I reminded myself that I had really lost him many years ago, somewhere along the Ho Chi Min Trail, when whatever he experienced was more than he could handle and he escaped through drugs and booze rather than peer directly into the heart of darkness as his father and grandfather had done and somehow survived, scarred and fragmented, barely intact.

Every year on Cathy's birthday I see the hope in her eyes whenever the phone rings and we're both thinking it might be Adam, and at Christmas we keep waiting for some message from him. So we go from year to year, never giving up hope, cherishing our memories of the bright, sunny boy we enjoyed for twenty years and struggling against the reality of never seeing our son again.

In some inexplicable way, I feel more connected to Adam when I come here to the Vietnam Memorial because this is the tangible monument to the war that destroyed him as surely as if he had been returned to us in a body bag and I could now read his name on this granite wall. *Adam Carver* would be embedded with over fifty thousand other names of young men and women who were sacrificed for presidential pride or stubbornness. My rage is compressed here—focused sharply on those leaders, the career politicians and policy wonks, who errantly and callously sentenced all these young people to death or, worse, to a living death, like Adam.

I remember the first time I visited this memorial, amidst all the controversy surrounding it—primarily that it wasn't grand enough—and I wanted to see for myself. What I found on that first visit, and all my subsequent visits, was that this memorial was unlike any other monument to previous wars: modest rather than monumental, personal rather than generic; emotionally gripping rather than visually awe-inspiring. It doesn't glorify war; it reduces it to the personal sacrifice that individuals have to make.

It translates patriotism from a hollow rhetorical shell to a deeply cherished inner belief. It assumes nothing and shows everything.

The simple design of a low-granite wall is unassuming even from a short distance. It is shaped almost like a boomerang—appropriately, I always think, because while it might take you outside of yourself at the outset, it doubles back to suck you deeply into a personal recognition of the unbearable costs of war. Because the wall maintains a low, even level against the horizon, it is deceptive, for it expands downward rather than upward and the paved walkway in front of the wall has a gentle, descending slope.

No more than two feet high at the beginning when you approach it, you read one name etched in the granite. As you proceed slowly down the inclined path, the names multiply, until you reach the mid-point where the wall is now high above you and the names are crowded together, like corpses gathered up after a battle. At this point you realize that you are surrounded by thousands upon thousands of the names of sons and daughters, brothers and sisters, husbands and wives, mothers and fathers, loved ones and treasured friends, calling to you in mute testimony to bear witness to the true cost of this hegemonic war. This gently sloping path has been a descent into hell.

In this place the dead mingle with the living. All around me I see the people connected to these sacrificed men and women paying tribute to their lost ones: mothers with children; older couples; bearded, pony-tailed veterans in army fatigues. The scene is a shifting kaleidoscope of action as people kneel in prayer, weep silently, leave flowers, make an etching of the loved one's name or take pictures of the family in front of this wall of remembrance. But to me this is also a wall of national arrogance and shame.

Who can forget the pitiful scene marking the war's final chapter? When the last American helicopter lifted off that roof in Saigon, its whirling blades screeching indifference to the abandoned souls stretching their pleading arms futilely toward its departing silhouette, what had been accomplished to justify the loss of so much life—our "national treasure," as politicians like to say in pious tones, attempting to mask their callous indifference? In my mind, nothing!

I walk slowly past my fellow mourners and up the inclined path to the other end of the memorial where the wall is once again reduced to its smallest height with only a few names inscribed. All the while I'm talking to my son and telling him that whether his name is here or not, this is his confederacy of comrades who marched off to yet another war in dutiful obedience, mindless of the ultimate price they would pay in death or shattered lives, and he and they are all deserving of full honor. My mental communion, while not cathartic, brings me a sense of completed duty.

I stand at the edge of the wall for a moment, collecting my thoughts for my return to the superficial peace of ordinary life, when off in the near distance I see a heavyset black woman, her hands covering her face, her body shuddering uncontrollably. Quickly, acting purely on impulse, I move to her side and wordlessly I touch her arm. She removes her hands from her tear-streaked face and looks at me with an expression of bottomless anguish.

"My son..." she says, taking big gulps of air and looking off towards the memorial, "My son don't got his name on that wall but he died over there just as sure as if he'd got himself killed."

She pauses and then looks at me. Something in my eyes must convey a kindred sadness because she continues. "Came back from there a drug addict and no matter how hard he tried, he just couldn't lick it." Her voice rises to a wail. "Now he's dead from an overdose, leavin' a wife and two babies."

I see the tears spilling from her eyes again and instinctively I move into her, wrapping my arms around her and drawing her towards me. She accepts this overture and lays her head on my shoulder, weeping softly. We stand huddled together in the cool morning air, two strangers suddenly bonded by our intimate grief, mourning the living and the dead.

Urgent Love

"Let's get married," he says impulsively, his arms around the naked body of the girl lying quietly in the bed beside him--the girl he met just a week before. The words pop out of his mouth in a mindless rush, like scurrying mice, and he waits in the sheer blackness of their motel room, not breathing, for a response. He feels her hand tighten on his chest, her fingernails lightly grazing his flesh; then her head rises from the pillow and he senses, more than sees that her face is directly above his. When she finally speaks, her voice is low and heavy.

"What?"

He repeats, "Let's get married."

She emits a throaty laugh, deep and unguarded. He loves the way she laughs and she laughs often. She seems full of laughter and high spirits.

"What made you say that?" she asks, not sounding angry or belittling, but curious and amused.

"I love you," he says softly, not quite believing his own impulsiveness.

"You love me?" She repeats his sentiment as a question.

"Yeah!" he says with more authority as his mind wraps around the idea and he becomes more comfortable with it.

"But we just met!"

"I know, but you're special...someone I'll dream about back in Iraq."

"Oh," she says, patting his chest, "we know so little about each other."

"What do I need to know?" he says with conviction. "I'm twenty; you're eighteen. I'm Polish; you're Swedish. I'm Catholic, not practicing; you're Lutheran, not practicing. We both like pizza and dancing and Eminem and Iggy Pop and Cream and roller coasters and the beach. We both like a good time." He pauses. "We're great in bed together."

She interrupts him with, "Where we've been most of this week."

"Okay," he says, chuckling and squeezing her shoulder, "and you're on your own. My Mom's dead. My father's a drunk. We really don't have anybody."

She listens to his description of the two of them while gently tracing with her finger the scar across his chest from the shrapnel wound he received on his last tour of duty. "A roadside bomb," he had said when she discovered it on their first night together, just six nights ago, and she could tell that he didn't want to give any more details.

When he listed what he knew about her and said, "You're on your own," that was, she reflects, true. But she hadn't told him why she was alone: the pregnancy at sixteen and the abortion; her disapproving parents' disowning her and her flight to the city; the waitress job and dreary boarding house; the stream of soldiers from the nearby army hospital as she drifted mindlessly from one man to the next, fueled with alcohol and pot and pills, carried along on a cloud of laughter and good times and casual sex. She had never been proposed to, never thought of marriage, never gave much thought to the day after tomorrow. Now here was this very cute boy with the sad, dark eyes and those beautiful lips and strong arms, who really knew his way around a woman's body, and he was so generous with his money, and he wanted to marry her.

This unexpected turn in her life is appealing if for no other reason than it gets her off the endless merry-go-round and turns her in a new direction. She speculates briefly on a different life as a married woman to a soldier.

He'd be overseas, of course, leaving for Iraq in just a few weeks, and they'd write long, sweet letters to each other and they could quickly find a nice apartment before he left that she could fix up and make it pretty so when he came home, he'd be surprised. It would be nice to have someone special in your life, she thinks, smiling in the blackened space between them. He was so cute and they got along so well and he was a good lover. And then, of course, there would be more money, and she'd be Mrs. Peter Dumbrowski..

She says the name again to herself. She isn't sure how he spells his last name, but it has a nice ring to it as she silently repeats it a third time. Yes, why not? she thinks; it might be fun!

"You're really serious?" she asks, confirming his intent, now that the idea was growing in appeal to her.

"You bet I am!" he says, growing more enthusiastic, and the more he says it, the more convinced he is that his audacity is leading him in the right direction. No guts, no glory, as they said in the army. Still holding her, he looks up at the invisible ceiling and speaks as if to himself.

"It would be so great to have someone to come home to. Iraq is a stinking hellhole! Hot and filthy and..." He pauses, struggling for a way to express his next intimate thought. "...and a guy can get really down in the dumps at the end of a day. You've been out on a mission with all the heat and dust and all the shit going down around you -- all around you -- and seeing bloody bodies, sometimes the Iraqis, sometimes American, sometimes your buddies or soldiers you saw in camp that morning."

She feels his grip tighten around her and his voice rises almost to a shout. She struggles to see the contours of his face but the blackness is impenetrable.

"And you go out every fuckin' day, followin' orders to take this street! Secure this area! Search this row of houses! You're never sure who's the enemy or where he is. You never know if this is the day when your number's up. Maybe it'll be your bloody body that other soldiers will pick up and bring back to the base."

He pauses, still staring at the invisible ceiling, and he feels her gently kissing his trailing scar. Then he turns and encircles her in his arms, now speaking in a softer voice, and she's aware of his warm breath puffing against her face.

"The guys who have wives or sweethearts, they can get things off their chest. It helps a lot, you know, when you can share what you're feelin' with someone. Even if it's only in a letter. We never talk about it with other guys. Some guys get really torn up inside. They go off their rocker or go cryin' to the chaplain. That's not for me."

He pauses, and when he speaks again his voice is raw and intimate. "I'd like to share things with you."

He squeezes her soft, plump body and kisses her on the nose.

"So what do you say?" he asks quietly, a tinge of uncertainty creeping into his voice.

She feels secure in his strong arms, with the tattoos on his shoulders and forearms, and she nuzzles against his lean body in a comfortable rather than sexual way. The blackness of the room now seems to be broken with a fuzzy light encircling their coupled bodies and she feels lightheaded.

"Yes," she whispers.

"What?"

"Yes, I said yes," and she giggles

"You will?" he asks, not quite believing her answer.

"Yes, I will!" she says in a louder voice, laughing and pushing against his body.

He resists her pushing away and draws her closer to him, his lips seeking hers. Their bodies mesh and his kisses become more urgent.

"So nice! So sweet!" he murmurs, and she responds, "Yes. Yes," and the room's blackness, seeping out into the world, is, for the moment, kept at bay.

When he slips into her, she realizes that for the first time he isn't using a condom. The prospect of another pregnancy pops into her head with alarm at first, but then an entirely new notion floats across her brain: motherhood. Why not? It would be nice to have a little girl that she could dress like a little doll and who would love her and her alone. Of course, the baby would love her father when he returned from Iraq. And with a baby he'd have a real family to come home to; a real reason to stay with her. Yes, it could be fun! Then she thinks that he must be thinking the same thing. Why else would he have not slipped on a condom as he was so careful to do with all their other marathon lovemaking romps?

Now there's a whole new dimension to their sexual frolicking, and she eagerly moves her hips to the rhythm of his, as they play like two children delighted in the affirmation of their fantasies. She again feels, rather than sees, a warm light encircling their gyrating bodies and instantly feels giddy and secure.

She suddenly has a stray thought: I wonder when his birthday is?

Any Place Like This

He awakens early after a night of bad dreams and intermittent sleep. The first rays of a scorching July sun are already invading the room and extending tentacles across his bed. The sheets are damp from perspiration and he lies staring at the ceiling, momentarily confused by his surroundings. Finally, everything comes into focus.

He's back home in his own room—the room he grew up in and left to go to war. The three years of his interrupted life is now ended and he's back on track. He lifts his head and surveys the room's contents, reassuring himself that everything is real: the small desk by the window with the goose-neck lamp; the Shaker-style bureau where he carved his initials on the side when he was seven; his old set of dumbbells neatly arranged in the corner next to the closet, reminding him of his rigorous exercise regimen as he prepared for each high school football season. Everything is as he remembered it, yet slightly different, somehow much smaller than how he repeatedly pictured it while he was in Vietnam.

He studies the posters tacked to the wall of the rock bands and sports heroes he idolized as a kid. His gaze falls on the framed picture of his high school varsity football team. He sees himself in the first row, left, and scrutinizes that smiling, transparent face as though it belonged to a different person. Automatically his hand comes up and traces the shrapnel scar zigzagging from his forehead down across his right cheek, ending in the twisted upturn of one side of his mouth. The blameless face in that picture is gone forever, he thinks, not with sadness or anger; just a shallow resignation.

The doctors and plastic surgeons had worked on him through endless operations, but the deep scars, the distorted right side of his mouth and the drooping right eye could not be erased.

"We've done the best we could," the head doctor had said bluntly before his discharge from both the army hospital and the army, "but you must remember that half your face was blown away."

His glance moves across the team picture to Jim Camby standing in the second row, far right. Big Jim as everyone in town called him because he was six feet five by the time he was fourteen and built as sturdy as the base of an oak tree. Big Jim, with his shock of unruly black hair betraying his quarter-Indian blood; his broad, guileless smile and an air of happy, complacent satisfaction (never arrogance) that always surrounded him.

He forces himself to look away from the picture as thoughts dark and hurtful flood his brain. He turns over on his stomach and buries his face in the pillow, seeking to clear his head of all thoughts. What was it the army psychiatrist said? Focus on the present. Take one day at a time.

He hears his mother downstairs in the kitchen and knows she's making a big breakfast to welcome him home. **Focus on the present! Take one day at a time! Focus on the present!**

He rises from the bed and goes to his bureau where he quickly selects a polo shirt and a pair of folded jeans. The clothes slip on easily and now fit loosely since he's lighter now than when he left home. He slides into a pair of loafers from the bottom of his closet and crosses the upstairs hall to the bathroom. Avoiding looking at himself in the medicine cabinet mirror, he washes his face and brushes his teeth, then walks to the top of the stairs. He repeats his mantra: **Focus on the present!**

He quickly descends the stairs, passes through the dining room and into the kitchen where his mother is setting the table. He notes the fresh flowers from her garden, arranged in a small vase at the center of the table.

"Good morning, Drew," she says cheerfully as she extends her arms and rushes toward him. The faint odor of shampoo, coffee and bacon accompany her embrace. He gratefully accepts these comforting arms from the past.

She cried last night when she met him at the bus—the only person to greet him—and he read in her eyes the shock of seeing his distorted face. She insisted that he drive home while she chatted nervously and he knew that she was stealing glances at his scars.

He drove slowly and looked out upon streets and houses and other landmarks of his small home town as if he were visiting it for the first time. This town that had formed the background for his family history, his growing up, his father's death when he was seven, his play time and work time and dreaming time, his friendships and attitudes and aspirations, now seemed to him strangely different. It was like he had only seen it in black and white before and now he was viewing it in full color. Yes, it was like something you'd see in a movie. For all the years he had lived here, he now felt like a stranger, like he didn't belong.

"What are your plans for today?" his mother asks as she serves him a plate heaped with scrambled eggs, bacon, very crisp just the way he likes it, and hash-brown potatoes.

"I thought I'd go see Mr. Perry about getting my old job back," he says, reaching for the stack of toast on the table.

"So soon?" his mother says. "Why don't you take a little time off? Just relax."

"Mom, I had plenty of time to relax in the hospital," he says, a note of bitterness creeping into his voice. "I want to get back to some kind of normal life, and the sooner, the better."

He sees the confusion on her face and recognizes that the son who had gone off to war is not the same person who returned. She was struggling to adjust as much as he was. They had always been close, especially after his father died and there was just the two of them. Now they were eyeing each other cautiously, looking for a way back into that tight circle of casual love. It would take time.

He wants to explain to her that free time is now his enemy—the fertile ground for horrific memories, dark thoughts and self-pity, depression and rage. But he can't approach this topic without calling up those emotions and revealing how unsteady he feels at this point. Not now! Maybe later when things get back to normal. Maybe not even then.

"Can I use the car this morning?" he asks, buttering his toast and sending his mother a reassuring smile.

"Of course," she answers, happy to return his smile and keep things on an even keel, everything normal.

He sees that whenever she looks at him directly, she glances away quickly, sometimes with misty eyes. Yes, it will take time. Meanwhile, **focus on the present; take one day at a time.** He avoids more talk, his head bent over his food, eating quickly

"That was great, Mom," he says, scooping up the last bite of egg. "I really missed your cooking."

She chuckles contentedly as she carries dishes to the sink.

"Well, I'm off," he says.

She turns and gives him a fierce hug. "Give my regards to Mr. Perry," she says as he reaches for the car keys on the hook by the back door. "Will you be home for lunch?"

"Don't know, Mom. Maybe."

"Okay. I'm making your favorite meal for dinner: meatloaf, mashed potatoes, corn and chocolate cake. The usual time."

"Great!" he calls and he is out the door.

As he backs the car out of the driveway, he sees Mr. Bascomb, their next door neighbor, mowing his lawn. Mr. Bascomb spots him and pauses for a moment, offering him a slight smile and a small wave before resuming his mowing. No Welcome Home! No How Are You? Just a brief, glancing gesture from thirty feet away. Then he remembers what an ardent opponent of the war Mr. Bascomb had been and how he had tried ferociously to dissuade him from joining the army when he was called up

"Don't get yourself involved in this stinking mess, Drew," was how Mr. Bascomb has said it. "Be a conscientious objector. Go to Canada. Act crazy when you report to the draft board." When all Mr. Bascomb's talk of imperialistic impulses, capitalistic expansion and false war premises failed, disgustedly he had said, "Go ahead, be another killing agent for the greedy, arrogant oligarchs," and stormed out of the house.

Now it seemed as if the entire world agreed with Mr. Bascomb and the clamorous demands to end the war in Vietnam rise from nearly every segment of the U.S. population, with few dissenting voices. Returning soldiers like him, he had heard, were not greeted as patriots or heroes but were ignored, if not openly condemned and shunned. Hearing about all this opposition to the war while still in Nam shocked him and his buddies.

Every day they were putting their lives on the line for what? He loved the guys in his platoon with an intensity that transcended any feeling he had ever known before. They were his band of brothers, willing to die for one another and committed to never letting a wounded or dead comrade fall in the enemy's hands. With their adrenalin wildly pumping, their senses on full alert, the platoon's ferocious link of each man for all was what kept them narrowly focused during the day.

The nights were different. He was twenty-one and he lay in his bunk at night, always damp from the moist, suffocating heat, struggling to pierce through the confusion that surrounded him. Despite his exhaustion, he couldn't turn off his dark thoughts; couldn't retreat into the numbing solace of sleep, even with pills. He fought against accepting the meaninglessness of his sacrifice; against surrendering to the imminence of death that engulfed him; against questioning the love of country that motivated him or the commitment to duty that guided him.

This nagging mental conflict, when added to the mortal danger of daily combat and the physical deprivations of army life, gradually sapped his spirit and left him in a permanent limbo of morose, robot-like responses, ended only with a red-hot explosive burst and the startling, searing pain of metal devouring his face. Then, oblivion.

Now he was home, confronted by all the Mr. Bascombs, stirring all the suppressed resentment and confusion and rage he now had to struggle with again.

* * * *

It was only a ten-minute drive from home to the town center—a main street of four short blocks housing all the stores in the community. He parks the car in front of Perry's Lumber and Hardware Store. Mr. Perry had put up a big, new shiny sign since he left. Somewhere down the street a car backfires. Instantly, every nerve in his body is vibrating as he automatically looks for cover. Then, realizing where he is, he forces his body to relax.

He enters the store and the smells of metal tools and nails and, from the rear, newly cut lumber, makes him feel at home. Images of his life before Nam come flooding back to him.

He had worked for Mr. Perry since his sophomore year in high school, first in the lumber yard, unloading and stacking lumber. Then, when Mr. Perry saw what a conscientious worker he was, he was promoted to helping customers in the lumber section. When he finished high school, he had no thought of going to college since he needed to make some money to help his mother. Mr. Perry, who was getting old, offered him a full-time job as assistant manager and moved him to the front of the store.

"Personal attention and service is what keeps our customers coming back," Mr. Perry would say periodically. "Otherwise, they could drive twenty miles down the road to the big chain stores. Don't forget that, Drew."

He didn't forget and offered a warm greeting and a flashy smile to everyone he serviced. He had been voted "best looking boy" by the girls in his graduation class who described him in the yearbook as "the boy with the dreamy eyes." He always dressed neatly for work in a crisp white shirt, sharply creased slacks and shined shoes. He kept his wavy black hair short, defying the trend for long, tangled manes that his peers were sporting. He liked his job, liked dealing with customers, most of whom he knew by name, liked having adult responsibilities, and liked being a respected member of his community.

He was taking care of his mother and going steady with Rachel, his high school sweetheart. Mr. Perry, a widower with two grown daughters and no son, was like a father to him and had promised him that in five more years when he retired, he, Drew, could run the business. He was content with his life and his future and would have gone on in his happy niche but for the escalating war in Vietnam and the draft and the low number he drew. Then life took an about-face and kicked him in the ass.

He was yanked out of his tranquil little world, sent twelve thousand miles away to a swampy, snake and bug infested, unbearably hot and humid hell and told to kill, kill, kill! Or be killed. A clearly primitive equation: the gooks or him.

Still, from all the speeches the army had delivered in boot camp and before shipping him over to Nam, at first he had felt he was serving his country in a noble cause. Then everything turned sour and the whole country seemed to be turning against the war.

Rachel remained loyal for six months before announcing in a Dear John letter that she was engaged to Joey Markham, son of the local Ford dealership owner. Then his mother sent him a clipping from the local newspaper announcing the death of James Camby, known to everyone as Big Jim, in a surprise attack by the Vietcong. He knew Big Jim was in Nam but they had never run into each other. Now Big Jim was gone, and death's reality took another turn of the screw. When his moment came in the form of an exploding rocket grenade, he had cheated death but would bear the visible scars of that encounter forever.

"Drew Brody?" a voice from his left side—his intact side—calls, interrupting his thought stream. He turns to see a young man whom he vaguely remembers from high school but who was not in his class. Now he sees the look on the young man's face shift instantly from smiling composure to startled shock as his eyes pop and his jaw goes slack. *A thorough confirmation of the effect my appearance has on people*, he thinks as he forces a smile, knowing that this facial movement exaggerates his already distorted features.

Momentarily speechless in his discomfort, the young man finally says, "Hi," weakly extending his hand. "I'm Josh Cooper. I was on the JV football team when you were on varsity," he explains as an introduction.

"Hi Josh," he says, nodding his head as if he remembers.

"When did you get back?" Josh asks, still with unsettled features.

"Yesterday. Is Mr. Perry around?" he asks quickly, not wishing to prolong Josh's clear discomfort.

"Yeah. Yeah. He's in his office."

"Thanks," he says, avoiding another smile, and heads toward the small office in the back of the store. He knocks and hears the familiar, high-pitched voice say "Come in!" He opens the door and pauses at the threshold.

Mr. Perry is sitting behind a large, cluttered desk, examining some bills, and, at first, doesn't raise his head to look at his visitor. His heavy gray hair falls over his forehead, brushing the black rim of his thick glasses. His slight frame seems to have shrunk in the last few years. Then he looks up with his keen brown eyes and stares directly at him.

"Jesus Christ!" he says loudly, dragging out both words in one long escaping breath. "Jesus Christ!" he says again, this time not as loud or as elongated. A shifting battery of emotions flickers across his face like a fast moving thunder storm and, just as fleetingly, disappears, replaced with a forced smile.

"Drew. Drew," he says, rising from his desk and coming forward with a brisk stride and arms extended wide. A mutual embrace with slaps on the back is genuine on both sides but ends quickly in awkward shyness.

"I didn't know you were back," Mr. Perry says, returning to his chair and motioning him to the one guest chair in the office. "When did you get home?"

"Last night," he answers, trying not to smile, but he is happy to see his old boss and mentor.

"Your Mom kept me up-to-date on your exploits." He pauses and his voice softens. "Sorry to hear of your injury." An awkward silence follows, ended by Mr. Perry. "But you're home now and that's what matters."

"I'm eager to get back to work," he says. More awkward silence.

"Sure! Sure! But don't you want to take a little time off, first? Maybe take a vacation? Do some traveling?"

"No, Mr. P," he says with an emphatic set to his jaw, using the special abbreviated name he had started using in high school.

Mr. Perry seems momentarily lost in thought.

"Okay, sure!" he says finally, smiling at Drew. "Josh Cooper has been working here since you left but he knew it was temporary until you came home. We've made quite a few changes in our inventory setup but Josh can stay on for a few weeks and fill you in. Why don't you start next week?"

"That's great!" he says and can't help smiling.

His old boss's face changes instantly, conveying deep sadness as his mouth turns down, his eyes cloud over and the lines in his cheeks deepen. Mr. Perry takes a deep breath, shoots up from his chair and practically races around his desk. He's talking rapidly.

"Okay, Drew. See you next Monday, 8 AM, usual time," he says cheerfully, clapping him on the shoulder. "By the way, I can start you with a small raise."

"Super, Mr. P," he says. "Thanks."

They shake hands.

"Give my best to your mother," Mr. Perry calls as he leaves the office.

"I will," he says and walks quickly through the store and out the front entrance into a glaring sun. The heat rising off the pavement hits him like a body blow, reminding him of the unrelenting heat in Nam. He stands still, adjusting his eyes to the bright light. He hears a small voice saying his name and turns to see Big Jim Camby's sister, Pam, a few feet away.

"Hi, Pam," he says, without smiling, for he's learned the startling effect his smiles have on people.

Pam quickly covers the few feet separating them and leans up and kisses him on his cheek—his bad side. She ignores the slight shudder of self-consciousness that whips along his shoulder as he tries to duck his head away from her gentle kiss.

"I didn't know you were home," she says in her soft, little-girl voice. She's shorter than he is, and in the blazing sunlight that gives her body a rippling, almost illusory effect, she looks delicious. She's wearing white shorts and a pretty blue halter-top and open-toe shoes. Her hair, honey blond, glistening in the sunlight, is short and brushed back from her forehead in natural waves. Her face, with wide-set brown eyes, a broad turned-up nose and a full mouth, set in pale, translucent skin, has an innocent, fresh-scrubbed appeal, as does her smile which is warm and guileless. He takes her all in with unexpected pleasure and does a quick mental calculation that she must be eighteen now since she was three years behind him and Big Jim in high school.

"It's so good to see you," she says, radiating warmth, and for a moment he forgets his current appearance and flashes back to a time when she was his best friend's little sister who harbored a crush on the varsity quarterback. He accepted her adulation and tolerated her with bemused indulgence.

"How you been?" he asks.

"Good," she answers. "I'm off to college in the fall and trying to get everything settled at home."

He remembers that she's the only remaining child.

"How's your mother?" he asks.

For the first time she looks away from him, gazing down the street. "She suffered a stroke shortly after my brother died and is bed-ridden now," she says, all in one breath. "Her sister, my Aunt Cora, came to live with us. She's a nurse and takes good care of Mom. She's a blessing. Of course, I'll be home on weekends to help out."

She looks up at him again and smiles that wide, warm smile that melts him. She's looking intently at his face now, and he can feel his color rising.

"You must have suffered a lot of pain," she says with a child-like directness that startles him. But her clear brown eyes show no fright, no revulsion, only compassion. He meets her steady gaze, saying nothing, feeling that somehow she intuits everything—that this young woman with her appraising, caressing eyes has an expansive, ancient soul. He feels comfortable, peaceful for the first time since coming home. He allows himself a smile and her expression never changes. Finally, she breaks her thoughtful gaze.

"I've got to get out of this heat. How about buying me a cherry coke at the diner?" she says, laughing easily. He eagerly agrees.

They quickly walk the one block to Skelly's Diner. As they slide into a booth, he's aware of the prolonged stares they're getting from the other customers and the two countermen. The waitress knows Pam, greeting her by name and sending a forced, fleeting smile in his direction before looking away. While he orders two large cherry cokes, she looks only at Pam.

"I read the wonderful letter you sent my mother from Vietnam after Jim's death," she says abruptly as the waitress beats a hasty retreat. "You two never got to meet up over there, did you?" Again she's fixing him with a steady, uncompromising gaze that, oddly, comforts him.

"No," he says. "Different assignments. Different areas."

Now she looks down at the salt and pepper shakers at the end of the table. "The hardest part of all..." she says, stops, swallows, breathes deeply and starts again. "The hardest part of all was learning that it was friendly fire. A rocket from a helicopter that thought it was firing on the Vietcong." She pauses again. "Killed Jim and three other Americans."

"Yes, I heard," he says quietly. "You'd be surprised—that happens a lot."

Her voice is tentative, wistful. "I don't know...," she says, returning her gaze to him. "Now it all seems so meaningless, so senseless."

They stare in mute understanding, inhabiting a bubble of joint pain and dislocation, drawing them inexorably closer. The waitress brings their cokes and the spell is broken. As if reviving from a deep reverie, Pam shifts the conversation quickly.

"What are your plans now?" she asks.

He tells her about starting his old job next week, and the conversation flows easily from general topics about the town and their mutual acquaintances from high school, to her college scholarship at the state university and her plans to be a teacher, and his future at the store when Mr. Perry retires in a few years. The casual intimacy, the ease of sharing unguardedly, spontaneously, makes them linger, delighted in each other's company, for a second round of cokes followed by burgers and fries. An hour and then another half hour pass quickly and finally she says she must get back home.

"I'd like to visit your mother," he says casually, hoping she'll invite him now, but she looks pensive before replying. "Drew, I don't know if that's a good idea." He looks puzzled and she continues. "I mean, she's in a very delicate state of mind right now, and seeing you, Jim's best friend, might just be too much for her. Revive too many old memories; bring up a lot of old grief."

He sees the persuasive logic of her argument and nods his understanding. He moves on to the more important issue.

"I'd like to see you again," he says, suddenly feeling awkward for the first time since he met her on the sidewalk. She throws him a generous smile and touches his arm. "Anytime you like," she says and he knows she means it. "We still have the same number," she adds encouragingly. "You must have it memorized from all the times you and Jim called each other."

He throws his head back and, unmindful of how he looks, he laughs. "I do."

He walks her back to where her car is parked. She opens the driver's door, turns abruptly and kisses him on the cheek—again the bad side—and says, "Don't forget to call me," As she slips into the seat, her shorts ride up and her bare, beautifully shaped legs angle up toward the pedals. Her full breasts are more exposed from his standing position and he is instantly smashed with desire.

He moves to the sidewalk and they both wave before she drives off. He stands as if in a trance, reliving, relishing each glorious detail of this chance encounter. Finally he remembers that he promised his mother to pick up some light bulbs, and he walks back to Mr. Perry's store.

No one is visible when he enters the store, and he makes his way to the back, to the shelves where the light bulbs are neatly stacked, a few feet away from Mr. Perry's office. The office door is partially open, and although he can't see in, he hears Josh Cooper's voice.

"It's going to be awfully hard for customers to deal with him, with his face all disfigured like that. I mean, you could lose a lot of business."

He's reaching for a pack of sixty-watt bulbs as he hears this and his body locks, his arm, extended toward the bulbs, freezes.

The air grows thick around him and the light seems to dim. Then he hears Mr. Perry's high-pitched voice, coming fast and angry.

"Let me tell you something, Josh. Drew Brody was sent off to fight in a war that I, and a lot of other people, don't believe in. But he went and now this is the consequence. And if the people of this town, who have known Drew all his life, can't appreciate the sacrifice he's made and can't stand to face what this war does to our young men, then I don't want their business."

"Okay, Mr. Perry, you're the boss," Josh answers defensively. "I was only thinking of the store."

"Well, think a little less about the store and a little more about Drew," Mr. Perry says, sarcasm creeping into his tone. "He's going to resume all his duties as Assistant Manager that he had before and that's the end of it."

He doesn't want Josh or Mr. Perry to see him so he quietly moves away, forgetting the light bulbs, and slips out the front door. Once more the heat of the mid-afternoon delivers a wallop but his mind is racing, filled with jumbled thoughts that slowly form a clear pattern.

The soldier's courage he struggled to summon every day to face the life and death challenges in Nam didn't end with his coming home. His life was forever changed, and his courage to face the world's reaction to his living testament of the war's reality—and its wasted human toll—would be the greatest, longest test of all. But Mr. Perry's stirring words still ring in his ears, and he thinks of Pam Camby's open, honest heart and her unabashed kiss on his distorted face.

His fight would go on but he was not alone. Just as he had his buddies in Nam to watch his back, there were good people everywhere to look out for him and support him. He just had to **take one day at a time**.

Suddenly, he thinks of his mother and the meatloaf dinner she's making, and he's eager to get home.

Filtered Truths

"My god, he's chopping wood again!" she exclaims in the empty kitchen she has just entered, as she glances through the window over the sink and sees her husband agilely swinging the ax. She moves closer to the window and watches him, concern clearly visible on her face.

He works at a feverish pace, swinging the ax forcefully, expertly splitting the logs that had already been sawed into two-foot wedges. The split logs that fall off the tree stump he's using as a cutting block he angrily kicks a short distance away and quickly puts the next log in place. He's in perpetual motion, reminding her of some old speeded-up movie where the comic character frantically races about. She recalls that he's been like this for nearly two weeks, ever since they got the news of Keith's death.

Involuntarily, she flashes back to the afternoon when the two Army officers arrived at their home. Suddenly an ordinary day had become a momentous date of unremitting horror as they were quietly informed not only that their nineteen-year-old son had died in Iraq but that he had taken his own life.

Both she and her husband had sat in stunned silence upon hearing of Keith's death, momentarily unable to come to terms with the fact, but when the officer then told them it was a suicide, Tom shot up from his chair and shouted "That can't be true! No son of mine would ever do a thing like that!"

"I'm afraid it is true, sir," the officer said softly, glancing sympathetically at her. Tom rushed out of the room and then she heard the kitchen door slam. She remained sitting, immobile, and the silence was maddening loud. The officer offered some more stock phrases intended to comfort, but in this case, even in her state of shock, she knew they rang hollow because of the circumstances of Keith's death.

"Are you sure?" she asked, her voice cracking with disbelief. The officer interpreted correctly that she was referring not to Keith's death but to the suicide. Speaking again in a quiet, measured voice, the officer replied, "Yes, ma'am." Pulling an envelope from his breast pocket and offering it to her, he added, "Details of the investigation we conducted and the eyewitness accounts are contained in this report."

Without glancing at it, she took the proffered envelope and automatically placed it on the side table next to her chair. Her mouth felt dry and she was finding it hard to breathe. Numbness was creeping along her entire body and her mind was shutting down. She felt no inclination to cry or shout—that seemed too paltry a response to such overwhelming news-- but she was afraid that she would faint.

She rose from her chair and now she could vaguely remember thanking the officers and escorting them to the front door as the one man mumbled some more awkward stock phrases about duty and country and service and a grateful nation. As she opened the door, she had a sudden impulse to laugh but she knew if she started to laugh, she wouldn't stop and she'd be racked with deep, convulsive laughing spasms, totally inappropriate for the occasion.

Her vision became blurred as she closed the door and a hundred pinpricks of light were flashing behind her eyelids. Then she finally let go. Everything was floating away and she remembered seeing the wood floor rising toward her before the blackness set in, as she fell in a dead faint.

* * * *

Most of the ensuing two weeks had been mercifully taken up with all the arrangements for formal mourning. Both she and Tom decided not to meet the body at Anderson Air Force Base where all the dead soldiers' bodies were shipped back from Iraq. She was particularly adamant about that, resenting the hidden, dead-of-night manner that the government chose to keep everything away from the public's attention and downplay the human price of this war. Out of sight, out of mind. The body was delivered to Madden's Funeral Home, the one mortuary in this small Vermont town. Mr. Madden called them when it arrived and she drove into town to see her son. Tom refused to come.

"Mrs. Egan, I should warn you," Joe Madden said, his big sad eyes looking into hers when he met her at the back door of the funeral parlor, "…the bullet was discharged under his chin and went straight up, shattering facial bones and deforming his appearance."

She nodded mutely, recalling momentarily how Joe Madden's son had been in Keith's elementary class and was now off in college, while Keith….

He led her down a steep flight of stairs into a room that under harsh fluorescent lights seemed unbearably white. In the middle of the room was a gleaming steel table and on that table she saw the black body bag. She felt her legs growing numb and she staggered and would have fallen if Joe had not gripped her under her arm. The light was suddenly blinding and she struggled to breathe as they approached the black bag that was now filling her entire field of vision. A few steps away from the table Joe paused.

'Mrs. Egan," he said softly, "maybe you should wait until I have a chance to make Keith more presentable."

Her eyes never leaving the bag, she shook her head but knew if she said one word, she would fly out of control and collapse. Instead she consciously stiffened her knees and stood fixedly as Joe partially unzipped the bag and the blond hair and pale skin of her son came into view.

To her immense surprise, her mind seemed to snap into an objective, analytic mode, disengaged from her body. She gazed upon the features, noting the distortions. Evidently the trajectory of the bullet had caused one side of Keith's mouth to crumble, had crushed one cheekbone and blackened one eye. It looked like a harlequin mask rather than a grotesque testament to a moment of supreme despair, she concluded. Now she saw the small bandage at the top of the head where the bullet had exited. Then her mind floated back to her body and her thoughts became chaotic and her son's face became a silent, permanent scream for understanding.

She started to shake and a low keening sound exploded involuntarily from her throat, and she would have fallen against the table, collapsing on her son, if Joe had not grabbed her and gently led her away. Upstairs she signed a paper from the Army acknowledging the identity of the body, and the low wailing sound rose from the deepest recesses of her throat but she fought to suppress it.

She managed to say "My husband will call you about arrangements," and then she added, "Thank you," as she opened the back door, stepped out into the glaring sunshine and felt she was entering a world on fire.

When she arrived back home she had no recollection of her twenty-minute drive, and found Tom in the backyard, furiously chopping wood. He had already stored away over two cords— more than enough to last through the harshest Vermont winter— but since hearing the news he was either gone for hours tramping across the wooded countryside, clearly wanting to be by himself, or chopping, chopping, chopping wood.

She called her daughter, Jane—now her only living child, she thought, as she listened to the ringing at the other end in New York City where Jane was in graduate school—and quietly, in a rumbling voice that strived for firmness but erratically betrayed her, delivered the news of Keith's death. She heard Jane, who had always been very close to her brother, cry "Oh my god, NO!" and she gripped the phone tightly, focusing intensely on breathing, waiting for Jane's sobs to subside, refusing to join in her daughter's convulsive crying for fear of shattering into a thousand emotional pieces and never recovering.

When Jane's crying eventually subsided and she asked in a watery voice, "How did it happen?" she simply said "Suicide." There was total, extended silence on Jane's end of the line and then, in a voice weighted with anger and deadening in its finality, Jane said "I'm not surprised."

Little was said between her and Tom in the ensuing days, as each retreated to a separate world, struggling to make peace with the new reality. Tom's anger was just below the surface, ready to explode at any moment, while hers was deep, seething resentment against her husband, mingled with fits of anguish for Keith and regret that she could never reconcile father and son. They managed, somehow, to avoid recriminating confrontations, but at night, in the silence of their bed as each lay awake with neither daring to say anything, she longed for dawn's escape.

When the army officer called a few days after his visit to ask if they wanted a formal military funeral, Tom had answered the phone and replied curtly, "Definitely not. That would suggest he was a hero."

She and Tom had managed to discuss arrangements for Keith's funeral in the briefest of exchanges, stripped of consolation or remorse. No mention of Keith's suicide would be made to anyone. He died in Iraq, period. The coffin would be closed during the one-day wake at the Madden Funeral Home. A funeral Mass would be held in the Catholic church the next morning, followed by a private burial in the family plot where three generations of Tom's family had been laid to rest.

She had a vague remembrance from her Catholic elementary education about people who commit suicide not being allowed to be buried in consecrated ground, but she angrily dismissed the thought. Anyway, she was glad she had drifted away from a church that would not accept her son, and it was only on Tom's insistence that they would have a Mass.

The local paper published a brief obituary that she had written, saying "died while on active duty in Iraq." Their friends and townspeople sent condolence notes and emails and brought casseroles and pies and flowers to their door but, considerately, refused an invitation to come in for coffee.

Some of Keith's high school teachers sent notes saying what a special student Keith had been and how much they loved having him in class. Mr. Peterson, Keith's junior varsity football coach, wrote how much he admired the effort Keith brought to the game. This message evoked an angry response from her as she recalled how hard Keith had tried to please his father, a senior All-Star, by pursuing football, only to make second string on the junior team, to his father's unspoken but palpable embarrassment and displeasure.

A priest called, introducing himself as Father Duffy and wanting to know if they would like him to say the rosary at the wake. She said "No, thank you," with such conviction that he didn't question her further. She did say yes to the director of the high school choral group, Mr. Johnson, when he asked if the group could sing a few hymns at the wake, because she remembered how much Keith had loved singing in the school chorus and how close he had felt to Mr. Johnson.

Jane had stayed on for several days after the funeral, acting as a buffer between her parents. Tom was mostly silent around the house and escaped to his basement workshop, his woodpile or his long walks. He and Jane had enjoyed a close relationship when she was small, but when Keith came along, Tom seemed to divert all his energies and time to molding his son. When that effort proved frustrating and Tom's disappointment and ridicule of Keith pervaded their home, Jane, as a big sister, supported her brother against her father. Now Jane's barely concealed anger was an unspoken accusation against Tom which he tried to avoid.

In her anguish Jane also lashed out at her mother.

"Why didn't you protect Keith more against all that macho bullshit Dad was laying on him?" she asked in a fierce tone, startling her mother as they were cleaning up after dinner one night. Before she could even think of a response, Jane continued. "This whole business of volunteering for the army was just to please Dad, because he had volunteered for Viet Nam. It was Keith's desperate effort to be like him even though we knew that was impossible. Why didn't you intervene and talk him out of it?"

"Do you really think I could influence Keith against his father?" she asked, as old defeats came quickly to mind.

"Well, you could have tried," Jane protested. Seeing the tears welling in her mother's eyes, Jane took a conciliatory tone. "I'm sorry, Mother, but I just think all of this could have been avoided if you had stood up to Dad more."

"I did try, Jane," she said, aware that she was pleading with her daughter for understanding and feeling ashamed. Jane said "Yes, I know," in an offhanded manner and they finished their after-dinner chores in silence, the air thick with accusations. When Jane finally left, both her parents were not sorry to see her go.

* * * *

The day after Jane's departure, she went into Keith's room which had not been changed since he had left for the Army. She sat on the bed and looked about the room, focusing on individual items that reflected her son's short life. A framed copy of the poem he had written at ten that had won the local newspaper's poetry contest in the children's division. All through high school he had written poetry, encouraged and applauded by his English teachers but never shared with his father. Or with her, for that matter. It was only at his high school graduation when the principal mentioned that the town could boast of a gifted poet in their midst, did she and Tom learn of Keith's pursuit.

Tom was clearly embarrassed when the men at his local veterans' club now referred to Keith as "the poet," as did the men in his plumbers' union, and he started to refer sarcastically to "my son, the poet," when discussing Keith with her.

They were so unalike, she thought, and as time passed, she seemed helpless to bridge the gap between them. Tom loved fishing and hunting and had introduced Keith to these passions when Keith was very young, no more than six or seven.

"He's afraid of the fish," Tom reported with obvious disgust after returning from their first fishing outing, "and doesn't like worms."

"He's still very young," she protested, but Tom only offered a disapproving grunt.

The first hunting excursion that followed soon after was also a disaster. "He cried when I shot the deer and begged me not to shoot any more," was Tom's disdainful report. "He'd rather stay in his room and read than be with his old man."

Keith was a solitary child, she had to admit. He had learned to read early and developed a great love of books. He made friends easily but still seemed to enjoy spending afternoons after school reading in his room and, she now knew, writing poetry. She had recently discovered hundreds of poems stuffed into the bottom drawer of his desk. She read most of them. They dealt with typical adolescent themes, indicating a growing appreciation for nature and curiosity about the future and a longing for love. But sadly, she noted, too many dealt with alienation and vague references to feeling different which she had also ascribed to an adolescent phase and not understood. The last poem she had read was entitled **The Family**, and her hands trembled as she read the lines.

> My father sulks in silent disappointment,
> My mother soaks in quiet resignation,
> A question never asked but always thought,
> Who is this stranger in our midst?
> And I, too, feel the knotty wounds
> That can't be soothed or touched or kissed.

She was afraid to discover any more revelations of her son's appraisal of her and Tom, and she stuffed all the poems back in the desk drawer, resolving at some future time to approach them again, but now she knew she never would. Where had all of Keith's refined tastes come from: His love of opera and drawing and poetry? She acknowledged regretfully that he had seemed like a stranger to her, as well as Tom, and she had never understood or fostered his innate interests, primarily for fear of a wider gap between father and son.

She remembered the day he had come home from high school in an unusually excited mood.

"Mr. Johnson played a tape of the opera *Aida* for us today. Have you ever heard it? It's terrific!"

She smiled, not knowing how to respond except to say, "Better not mention it to your father. You know what he thinks about classical music."

She saw his enthusiasm deflate like a burst balloon. Then he quietly said, "But what do you think of *Aida*?"

She gave him a much weaker, embarrassed smile. "I think maybe I've heard some tunes from it," she confessed, "but opera is too high-faluten for me, I'm afraid."

Keith gave her a quizzical look, said nothing and went to his room. Soon, he was borrowing opera tapes from Mr. Johnson's collection and loud strains of swelling voices and orchestras were vibrating from behind his closed bedroom door, but only in the afternoon before his father got home from work.

The English prize at graduation and no athletic awards, so lavishly distributed in a town that seemed crazed with sports, was the final wedge between Keith and his father. She watched with a growing feeling of helplessness as Keith tried everything that summer after graduation to please his father. The more Tom withdrew, the more urgently Keith pursued him.

"Let's go fishing, Dad," he'd suggest as a weekend drew near.

"No," Tom would answer abruptly. "I wouldn't want to take you away from your poetry writing."

"If you're working on the boat engine, Dad, I'll give you a hand," Keith offered one Saturday morning, seeing his father carrying his tool box out to the driveway where his fishing boat was parked.

"No thanks. You were never interested in engines and now you'd only get in the way." Then, in a voice filled with quiet, deadly sarcasm, Tom Said, "Why don't you sit in your room and listen to opera."

She was watering the plants along the side of the driveway and was shocked to hear Tom's reference to opera because Keith only played the opera tapes when his father was out of the house. As if in answer to her unspoken question, Tom turned to her and said, "I met Rob Schneider in town the other day and the first thing he says to me was, 'you're raisin' a high-class son, Tom. Every time I deliver your mail in the afternoon, I hear all this high-tone opera blasting from your house and people bellowing away in some foreign language. Pretty fancy stuff!'"

Tom opened his tool box before adding, in deeply sarcastic tones, "So now the whole town knows that my son likes poetry and opera and you can bet I'll get a lot of razzin' about that down at the Veterans Hall."

She saw the crestfallen look on Keith's face as he turned and quickly retreated to his room.

"Why must you be so hard on him?" she said, half in anger, half in pleading.

"Is he a son I can be proud of?" Tom asked, his face a mask of frustration.

"Yes, he is!" she said adamantly. "He's smart and he's sensitive and he loves you and craves your approval."

Tom stared at her, as if he were weighing her estimation of Keith against his list of valued qualities. Finally he shrugged and, turning back toward his boat, said, "Maybe he'll write me a poem about his feelings."

"You'll drive your only son right out of this house," she shouted defiantly at his back but got no response.

From all their married years together she recognized Tom had always been the decision maker, seeking little input from her. Now she regretted that she had taken the easy path in deferring to him. She also recognized that he was a hard-working laboring man who had dropped out of high school halfway through his senior year to apprentice as a plumber and then had volunteered for the Marines when the Vietnam War flared up, postponing their wedding until he returned with a chest full of medals—a hero in their small, solidly conservative community.

The finished room in the basement that he had built for himself—he called it his man cave—was the sanctuary for the memorabilia of his life, all those things that reflected his personal identity as a man: his framed collage of war medals; his bowling trophies; high school football banners and posed pictures of him throwing a football; his gun collection; group pictures of his veterans' gatherings and snapshots of him in his Marine uniform marching in local parades on the Fourth of July and Veterans Day; more pictures of him holding fish or fowl or animals he had killed.

When she cleaned that room, she always noted the absence of any pictures of his family, but he was not a sentimental man, she reflected, except for these manly testaments. Then she would think of Keith's room with his neatly arranged writing desk and his secret stash of poems, his complete set of Shakespeare's plays that he had bought from his paper-route money while still in junior high, his pictures of his high school choral group on various field trips, and she would involuntarily shudder.

Separated by two flights of stairs, the worlds of father and son might just as well have been on different planets, she thought. A distance she had never found any way of bridging and, sadly, she had watched them grow further apart until Keith's final, desperate act of seeking his father's approval by volunteering for the Army.

"It's a good thing you didn't try for the Marines," his father announced when Keith broke the news. "You wouldn't make it through boot camp. The Army will take just about anybody." She saw the defeated look in her son's eyes and the shadows streaking across his face, but, caught up in her instant concern for his future safety, she had said nothing.

* * * *

She crosses the kitchen to the refrigerator, from which she takes eggs, milk, butter and bacon. She performs the rituals of preparing breakfast—filling the coffee maker, setting the kitchen table, toasting the bread, frying the eggs and bacon that he wants each morning for breakfast—all the while hearing the rhythmic thump of the ax as it cleaves through the logs and hits the top of the tree stump.

These and other daily routines are what hold her together, allowing her to float in a mindless state of numbness, keeping her from thinking too much and resenting her husband too fiercely. Having finished her preparations, she turns toward the kitchen door to call him to breakfast. She glances out the window and stops.

The morning sun spotlights his face and she observes his concentrated look as he furiously swings the ax, small beads of perspiration glistening on his brow. She squints in an effort to see more clearly, and now it is unmistakable: tears are streaming down his cheeks.

She decides not to call him and sits at the kitchen table, waiting for the door to open and the next interminable chapter of their lives to begin.

Reality Check

Michael met his father, a Green Beret, for the first time when he was six years old. No advance notice of this significant event was given because, as Michael's mother later explained, "I didn't want you to be disappointed if he didn't show up." Then, with a perceptible curl of her lip, she added, "That would have been just like him."

That summer day in 1971, Michael would always remember, was bright and muggy. He was playing in the back yard of the old Victorian house where he, his mother and Nana, his mother's mother, were now living in a rental apartment, two steep flights up in what had formerly been the attic. Michael had come to live with his mother in this small northern New Jersey town only a year earlier when she had gotten a job in a munitions factory, turning out armaments for the Vietnam War. Before that he had never lived with his mother but had been boarding with a number of families, some nice, some indifferent, in locations numerous and hazy so that he had no fixed sense of place or where he belonged.

During his boarding years, his mother would visit him most Sundays, bringing him a new children's book or a toy, wrapped in tissue paper and tied with colored ribbon to make it seem special. They would go for a walk and sometimes she would find a nearby diner.

"Let's have some ice cream!" she'd say excitedly, making it sound like a wonderful adventure. They'd sit in a booth and when the waitress came they'd always order two black and white ice cream sodas.

"Michael, that's impolite," his mother would say gently when he made loud sucking sounds with his straw as he tried to drain the last drop of syrupy soda from the bottom of his glass. He'd watch her examine her face in a mirror she drew from her bag and, satisfied with her appearance, put it back. Then she'd reapply her lipstick, dabbing it on the upper and lower lip and pursing her lips together for an even spread.

"You pay the bill," she'd say with a smile, handing him bills from her purse after looking at the check. Feeling very grown up and important, he'd take the check and the money to the counter where the cash register was and return with the change.

"We have to leave a good tip," his mother said, drawing coins from her purse and placing them on the table along with the change from the bill. "These people work very hard. I know! I used to be a waitress."

Occasionally Nana would be with them and they would dispense with their walk and just sit quietly in some corner of the house where he was boarding or, if the weather permitted, on a porch. During these joint visits, he was interrogated sternly by Nana.

"Are you saying your prayers?"

"Are you eating your vegetables?"

"Are you getting enough milk?"

"Has anyone hit you?"

"Do you change your underwear every day?"

"Do you wash your hands after going to the bathroom and before every meal?"

Whenever Nana questioned him, she had one eyebrow cocked and her lips, when not moving, were pressed firmly together, as though anticipating the worst. When Nana was present, his mother was mostly silent, nervously adjusting her bracelets, chain-smoking, crossing and uncrossing her legs and occasionally sending him quick, furtive smiles as his eyes darted between the only two relatives he had ever known. Nana's favorite expression to his mother, often repeated but mysterious to him, was "We're paying for your mistakes, Joy."

At the end of these Sunday visits, his mother would sweep him up in her arms, planting kisses all over his face, and he would cling to her fiercely. She always wore the same perfume and that unmistakable scent, mingling with the cigarette smell that clung to her hair and clothes, was immensely comforting to him. Then she'd place him back on his feet and smooth his hair with her hand.

"Be a good boy, Michael, and I'll see you next Sunday," she'd say with shining eyes and her broadest smile.

Nana would lean toward him, offering her rouged cheek to be kissed, saying nothing.

He'd watch them walk away, heading for the local bus or train station, his mother slender and tall in her high heels, and beside her, Nana, a short, stocky silhouette with her arm entwined with his mother's. He'd squint so he could see them as long as possible, until they disappeared in the distance. He hated the approaching dusk of short, winter Sunday afternoons, as if drawing a curtain between his wished-for life and his real life.

* * * *

Little family history was shared with him during his boarding years. He gradually came to learn that his mother was an only child whose father, his grandfather, had died in a sea disaster when she was four, and Nana, who had married late in life, had never remarried and raised his mother alone. His mother seemed much younger than the mothers in his boarding families, and he heard one of them say, "She's just a child," about his mother. When he asked about his father, his mother said, "Your father is a soldier fighting in a land far away."

"When will I see him?" he asked when he was four.

"Someday," his mother said, and her expression told him that this was all the information he was going to get.

In all his boarding homes, pictures of the parents' wedding were prominently displayed, but he had never seen any picture of his parents together and no mention was ever made of his father's relatives.

Most of the families he boarded with had the same family structure: mother, father and several children. With intense curiosity Michael watched these fathers interacting with their offspring. While all of them were away from home during the day, some of the fathers would play with their children at night, roughhousing with the boys and giving piggyback rides to the younger girls.

Sometimes fathers helped their children do homework, with everyone seated around the dining room or kitchen table. Books, papers, rulers, pencils and crayons were spread in a confusing welter, as young bodies twitched in nervous concentration, eyes rolling skyward and mouths haphazardly chewing on pencils. Other fathers seemed indifferent to their children, speaking only to the wife at the supper table and retreating to a comfortable chair to read the paper or watch television, before dozing off and being helped to bed by the wife.

While the ages of the children with whom he boarded varied widely, Michael was usually the youngest and lowest on the pecking order because of both his age and his status as a boarder. With those children nearest his age, whenever his play with them deteriorated into squabbles, they would vent their anger by calling him an orphan.

"You're not really part of our family," was the usual remark to which he remembered one angry little girl adding, "We'll be happy to see you go!" and her twin brother shouting, "Nobody wants you here!"

"I'm not an orphan!" he would angrily protest, but the rest of their belittling remarks cut to the bone, usually bringing tightlipped tears. He became acutely conscious of being an outsider, one who had to be on his best behavior at all times to be accepted; otherwise, he could be shunned, rejected, sent away.

Then one Sunday his mother arrived for her visit in a clearly excited state.

"Nana and I have found a nice apartment and you can live with us now and you'll have your own room!"

The prospect of living with his mother – he gave scant attention to Nana's presence in the prospective household – and, for the first time, having his own room, overwhelmed Michael with happy anticipation.

"When? When?" he cried, flinging his arms around his mother's neck.

She hugged him tightly.

"Just as soon as we get the place straightened up and buy a bed for you," she said, her voice crackling with excitement.

Then, spontaneously, they both did a little jig, holding hands, going round and round, his mother's laughter and his whoops of delight filling the room.

* * * *

In the months before his father's appearance, his relationship to his mother and grandmother grew in many dimensions as all three adjusted to their new and unfamiliar daily roles. Michael was in the first grade now and was away from home most of the day, except for holidays and school recess periods. Nana, he knew, had some unspecified problem with her heart and stayed home to take care of the apartment, prepare meals and supervise him when he wasn't in school.

In keeping with her own German upbringing – he now learned that she had been raised on a farm in upstate New York – Nana emerged as a strict disciplinarian and a dour presence. She performed all domestic tasks with glum resignation and responded to most of his boyish antics with stern admonitions. She seldom yelled or hit him, but she was never demonstrative or playful like his mother. She sighed a lot and seemed generally unhappy with her lot in life which, somehow, in unspoken ways, she managed to convey to him, was his fault. Michael was always wary of her and any scant love they shared was fostered through his mother's prodigiously affectionate spirit.

Nana's only respites from her life of dutiful drudgery were reading her Bible and watching the television soaps. *Days Of Our Lives* was her favorite, and no event, happy or catastrophic, was allowed to interfere with her viewing pleasure. When his mother came home from work just before supper, Nana would greet her with a litany of Michael's offenses for that day.

"He didn't make his bed this morning and he left the milk out on the counter when he had a snack after school and he ripped his shirt when he went out to play."

To these charges Nana would usually add complaints about nosey neighbors, troubles with local store employees, money worries or some newly emerging symptom of her poor health. His mother, clearly weary from a day on the assembly line at the munitions plant, would look off in the distance and say, "I'm sorry, mother," before turning to Michael and saying "You have to try to do better, son," all the while smiling wanly.

Supper, prepared and served by Nana, was eaten mostly in silence to avoid more of Nana's complaints. Then Nana would go off to watch more television and his mother would clear the table and wash the dishes while Michael dried them. They invested this daily chore with their own private ritual, invented by his mother. For each dish or utensil she handed him, he had to quickly name something that he had experienced that day, no matter how small or inconsequential, that had made him happy. Visually assessing the number of items in the sudsy sink, Michael would start with the grossest generalities: "Our nice home," or "My nice room," and "My comfortable bed," were his usual openers, followed by "A nice supper," and "My nice school."

As they moved from plates and serving dishes through pots and pans to cups, saucers and glasses and then on to knives, forks and spoons, his reflections on the day became more particular. Miss Daly, his first grade teacher, was always praising his work, which gave him bragging rights to impress his mother.

"Miss Daly said I was the best reader in the class."

"Miss Daly said I know all my numbers."

"We played tag at recess and no one could catch me before the bell rang."

"I drew a picture of a dog in art class and Miss Johnson showed it to the whole class."

"Frankie Parks and I are planning to build a fort tomorrow in the woods next to the cemetery."

Michael's listing of happy thoughts was interspersed with appreciative comments and encouraging smiles from his mother. As an incentive for him to keep searching for the good, the positive and the beautiful, his mother, whenever he was running out of particulars, would suggest additional categories for exploration.

"Did you see any beautiful scenery today?" she'd ask, or "What people did you meet today who were nice to you?"

These leading questions offered him goldmines of possibilities, allowing him to rattle off friends, neighbors, Big Al, the school bus driver, and Mr. DeMarco, the man at the local grocery store where Nana had sent him for bread. Then, switching to the pictorial mode, he'd describe scenes, like snapshots, of the orange sun burning through the snowy clouds, the white and gold church steeple against the dark gray sky, the white swans gliding on the brown pond in the town square, and the beautiful tiered wedding cakes on display in the window of Kutcher's Bakery.

If he succeeded in identifying a daily moment of conscious pleasure for each object that he dried, which, with his mother's assistance, he usually did, his winner's prize was sharing a small Hershey bar, eaten surreptitiously in the kitchen because Nana disapproved of chocolate as being bad for the teeth.

"One of my high school teachers," his mother was fond of telling him, "used to say that there are two ways of looking at life every day: the glass is either half-full or half-empty. You're a lot happier if you can see it as half-full."

Michael liked to hear his mother's recalling this saying, for he connected this positive attitude with her sunny disposition and tried to follow her example.

His mother would read him a story at bedtime, both of them side by side on his bed, propped up with pillows, or, sometimes, he would read one to her. Often, during his dramatic readings of stories he almost knew by heart, he would look up from the page to find her eyes closed and her head nodding.

"Do you like this story, Mom?" he'd ask in a louder voice, and her eyes would flutter open and she'd clear her throat and say, "Very nice, son. Go on!"

When it came time for the short prayers Michael said before going to sleep, they would both kneel by the side of his bed and she would say, "Remember to thank God for all the things that made you happy today," and then he'd crawl under the covers and wait for his good-night hug, which he'd return exuberantly. She'd flip the wall switch and close his bedroom door, leaving him in the darkened room, wrapped in a serene peacefulness. Before turning on his side in preparation for sleep, he'd add another prayer: "Please watch over my daddy, wherever he is, and bring him back home."

* * * *

It was Sunday. Nana had gone away on a day-long church outing and his mother was up in their apartment, ironing clothes. Having grown tired of a one-person game of marbles that he had concocted, Michael was sitting under the large oak tree in the back yard, daydreaming, when his mother called him to the back porch where she was standing next to a very tall, thin man dressed in a soldier's uniform with a green beret.

"Michael, this is your father," she said flatly and disappeared into the house.

Michael stood frozen at the bottom of the four steps leading to the porch and looked at the man's highly polished boots, numb with shock and too fearful to raise his eyes. The air had suddenly grown thick and sticky around his head. His mind was racing to absorb the staggering import of this moment but was quickly overwhelmed and shut down completely. He could feel a slight trembling in his legs as his eyes remained transfixed by those shiny black boots, like black holes sucking him into turbulent emotional confusion and indecision.

The silence, so seemingly interminable as to be painful, was finally broken by a baritone voice coming from somewhere above his head.

"Well, hello, buddy. I'm glad to finally meet you."

His voice choking, Michael barely managed to mumble "Hello," without moving his eyes from the boots. Now the boots were descending the four steps and a huge out-stretched hand came into his fixed field of vision.

"I'm your father," the soldier declared assertively, verifying his claim on Michael's attention and reinforcing the momentous news his mother had already announced.

Still confused and afraid to look up, Michael forced himself to lift his hand to meet the very large one extended towards him, and he watched his hand disappear inside the enveloping fingers in a grip that actually hurt.

"How are you, Mickey?" the voice boomed in a hearty, casual style, which Michael was unable to reconcile with the awfulness of this occasion.

Another barely audible one-word response escaped Michael's lips: "Fine." Then, his Nana's German discipline and his mother's gentle insistence on courtesy found him automatically adding, "Thank you."

His mind was starting to function again as he took note of his being called Mickey, a variation of his name that he had never heard before. As if reading his thoughts, the voice added.

"We decided to call you Mickey right after you were born because I'm Michael too, and that way, there wouldn't be any confusion."

Michael was digesting this information when the voice added a further clarification, "...since I'm Michael Senior and you're Michael Junior, but we didn't want to call you Junior."

More new information!

Words coming rapidly, the voice continued to elaborate on the topic.

"So this seemed like a good solution, but your mother wasn't crazy about 'Mickey' and your grandmother threw a fit."

Michael knew intuitively that by "grandmother," the voice meant Nana.

Except for the upward extension of his arm to complete the handshake, Michael remained rigidly stuck in the same place at the foot of the porch stairs, his mind grappling with the realization that these boots, this voice, this hand – all belonged to his father. Now his mind was screaming, "My father! Father! Father! MY FATHER!"

Suddenly the shiny black boots were coming down the porch steps and the torso and face came fully into Michael's view.

"Why don't we sit down?" his father said, motioning for Michael to join him on the top step.

Absorbed in discovering his father's physical appearance, Michael stood mutely, ignoring the invitation while his father continued talking. The man sitting at the top of the stairs had large brown eyes under arched eyebrows, a long thin nose and closely cropped black hair visible on that side of his head not covered by his green beret. The mouth was wide with narrow lips that curled upwards as he smiled, displaying beautiful teeth, white and even, set against a ruddy complexion. A long neck with a pronounced Adam's apple rested on broad shoulders and a long, spare torso. His changing expressions conveyed an open, exuberantly assured and robustly masculine countenance, dazzling his son.

His father patted the space next to him. Awkwardly, Michael shuffled forward and sat down on the step below where his father was sitting and his father's long legs jutted out past Michael's side. His father placed his huge hand on Michael's shoulder but exerted no pressure to draw the boy towards him.

"So how have you been?" he asked in a light, inquiring tone that Michael had so often heard neighbors use with each other, and he could not decode the question. Did he want a history of Michael's life as far back as he could remember? Did he mean, how was he doing presently? Did he mean, how was his health? Whenever Michael heard neighbors respond to this question, the conversations usually centered on health issues. Michael s mind weighed many possible answers but again he resorted to "Fine."

"Your mother tells me you're doing very good in school. What grade are you in?"

"I just finished first and the principal told my Mom that I was the best reader, and I can add numbers," Michael blurted out, surprised with his expansive answer.

"That's great! You must take after your Mom," he acknowledged and quickly moved to another subject.

"Do you like sports?" he asked.

"Yes," Michael said quickly and he could feel his diaphragm sinking back to its normal position and his breathing returning to a regular pattern. "I like to swim and dive and ice skate and roller skate and ride my bike that Mom got me for Christmas."

Michael looked at his father's face and saw a fleeting shadow of puzzlement.

"But what sports do you play?" he asked in a still jovial tone.

Michael was silent and momentarily confused, since he had just listed all the sports he liked. Sensing the boy's confusion, his father continued.

"Do you play baseball or football or basketball or hockey? I started playing those sports when I was your age. I'll bet you're a chip off the old block and even a better athlete than your old man."

Michael looked away from his father's face and gazed off into the distant recesses of the back yard as his mind weighed the situation. He sensed, somehow, that this was a crucial question and his answer would determine the subsequent flow of dialogue. Except for being included in two or three short, haphazard games of catch with his boarding families, he had never even owned a baseball mitt and had never played any of the sports his father had mentioned. He knew he couldn't fake it, although the temptation was ripe, because he knew so little about the rules and positions. Feeling that a simple "No" would be a vast disappointment to his father, he hit upon a strategy that might redeem himself in his father's eyes. Ignoring the question, Michael spoke rapidly.

"I like to go sledding in the winter. Last winter, a lot of bigger kids in the neighborhood were sledding down this steep hill in the cemetery and sailing over the big stone wall into the street. And they dared me to do it and I did. They couldn't believe it!"

Michael had delivered this testament to his bravery in one continuous exhalation of breath and was now gulping air back into his lungs and still not daring to look at his father's face.

"Have you ever been to a baseball game?" his father asked in a much less jovial tone.

Michael decided he had no options.

"No," he said in a barely audible voice.

"Have you ever gone fishing or hunting?" his father asked, and Michael, who had never even thought about these activities, heard the dreaded "No" escaping from his lips.

There was a long, awkward silence.

"Well, then, Mickey, what else do you like to do?"

This last question was uttered in such a casual way as to suggest indifference. Michael briefly reviewed the many activities that filled his days and felt that now he might regain lost ground.

"I love to read and draw and watch movies. I like to sing. I know the words of a lot of songs. I like to play with my toy trucks and my soldiers and I like to play cards. I play Go Fish with my friend Frankie, and Mom and I play Old Maid. I have a train set that we put up last Christmas and I made a snowy mountain out of cardboard and cotton."

Suddenly Michael was inspired to ask, "What do you like to do?"

His father gave a short laugh and, in a voice tinged with sarcasm, said, "Not any of those things, sport." He paused, then said, "My other son is only four but he's already hitting and catching a baseball like a pro and loves to shoot baskets."

This mention of another son threw Michael into total confusion and he stared silently down at the bottom step, trying to fit this statement into his known world. His father, seeing the boy's confusion, continued.

"I guess you didn't know you had a little brother…well, a half- brother actually, and a little sister too."

Brother! Sister! This stunning news echoed inside Michael's head, seeking some logical resting place. How could this be? All the families he had boarded with had more than one child and he saw how brothers and sisters could squabble among themselves but usually presented a united front against outsiders, including him. He had daydreamed about having a brother who would stick up for him and share his life, but he accepted this wish as fantasy. Now here was the announcement that he had a real brother. And a sister. Then he remembered the correction his father had made and he was confused again. What's a half-brother? He heard his father's voice again.

"You see, Mickey, your mother and I divorced about a year after you were born, and I remarried and have another family now. We live in Texas."

So many revelations in so short a span of time were overwhelming Michael, who could think of nothing to say because everything was jumbled and he needed time to wrap his mind around all these startling facts and to sort things out. Yet in the midst of his confusion, some primitive instinct bubbled to the surface of his brain: sibling rivalry. If he had a younger brother who did things that earned their father's admiration, he would have to compete. What was he really good at? He remembered an area that he had only touched on. Summoning all his courage, he looked up at his father.

"Would you like to see my drawings? Mom keeps all of them in a big folder. She says they're gorgeous. I can show them to you if you like."

Michael saw the dark expression sweep across his father's face and felt that he had made some mistake but he had no idea what it was.

"Gorgeous!" his father said with quick, explosive energy. "Gorgeous!" he repeated, elongating the end of the word into a hissing sound. "What kind of word is that?"

Michael briefly pondered this question with total bewilderment when his father quickly answered it.

"No man uses a word like that!" he said emphatically, turning his head away.

His father's visceral response shocked the boy. The hot, sticky air rose up to assault him again and he was paralyzed with confusion and self-loathing. He had no idea why that word had angered his father, but since everything he said seemed to alienate him further, Michael retreated to silence as his only defense.

"I need to use the john," his father said and abruptly rose and went into the house, banging the screen door.

Crossing his arms and laying his head on his knees, Michael listened to the footsteps as his father mounted the two flights of stairs to the attic apartment. All the windows were open to combat the summer heat and Michael soon heard the voices of his father and mother rising in pitch as snatches of words drifted down to him.

"...raising him to be a pansy...needs to be toughened up...talks like a girl." Then, in a mocking, singsong voice, "likes to read and sing and draw."

Michael buried his head between his knees and squeezed his hands into knotted fists. Still, he could now hear his mother's voice, loud and shrill.

"How dare you breeze in here after five years and think you have the right to speak like that about your son and to judge me! What do you expect when he's never had a father? He's a very smart, caring and sensitive little boy and that's no thanks to you. He's been through a lot because of your refusal to support him. I couldn't even give him a home until I got this job. He's been shuttled from pillar to post and you never gave a damn…too busy taking care of your other family, so forget about your first-born. You know what? I'm glad you haven't been in his life because I don't want my son to grow up to be like his father. You think you're such a man because you're a tough Green Beret. You're a disgrace! You don't know the first thing about being a man…a real man!"

She continued on, her words coming more rapidly, intermingling now with sobs. Michael jumped up and ran to the farthest end of the yard, crumpling under the large oak tree and giving vent to his frustration and tears. From this distance he could barely hear their voices but still he put his hands over his ears and closed his eyes to shut out the world, totally defeated. He stayed locked in this position for what seemed like a very long time when the slamming of the screen door invaded his benumbed isolation and he looked up and saw his mother hurrying towards him. Wordlessly, she slumped down beside him and encircled him in her arms. He buried his face in her lap and now the tears came uncontrollably, for he knew with certainty that his father had left.

"I know. I know," his mother kept repeating, softly stroking his hair.

"Why doesn't he like me?" he asked when he finally raised his head and looked at his mother.

She stared ahead, forming an answer and then, still holding and stroking him, she spoke in a level, firm voice.

"Michael, he doesn't know you. He couldn't see in such a short time what a bright and brave and talented boy you are. How you do everything I ask you to do and how you always tried to adjust to all those families I had to board you with, and what a kind heart you have, and how quick you are to see the good in people, and how you never complained when money was tight and I couldn't buy you things, or when we moved you to another family or another school. How funny you are! And loyal! And so creative!"

She paused as though weighing her thoughts and then proceeded in a darker tone.

"He's your father in name only, and you're still very young, but try to understand that to be a father, a real father, means taking responsibility and being with your son and guiding him and helping him to grow into a man." Then, in a deeper voice, she added, "Not someone who just shows up at your door one day and, having spent no time with you since you were a year old, expects his son to be just like him."

Brushing his hair back off his forehead and assuming a lighter tone, she said, "But not all boys have fathers, Michael, and you're strong and good and you'll have to do it on your own." Hugging him closely, she added, "I'm here for you, son, and Nana, too, but we're all the family we've got."

Suddenly, on sheer impulse, he asked, "Why did you and my father divorce?" trying to make sense of this adult puzzle. He had a vague understanding of divorce from other kids at school.

His mother sat motionless in silence for what seemed to him a long time before answering.

"We were very young, Michael, and you arrived very quickly, and after that I wanted to settle down but your father wanted adventure. It's hard to explain. We were just very different people and couldn't agree on anything. Your father joined the Army and wanted to make a career of it. We decided to part."

The sun had started its descent in the western sky and the branches of the oak tree they were sitting under now enveloped them in deep shade. A slight breeze drifted across the yard, drying the tears and perspiration on Michael's face. They sat silently, huddled together, as he struggled to weigh her words against the painful, confusing events of the day. So often he had longed for a father and dreamed of what he'd be like and fantasized about all the things they would do together. Now, in some undefined but strongly felt way, he recognized that these were, indeed, wishes, dreams and fantasies.

"Nana won't be home 'til late and I'm going to make supper now, and you can have anything you like," his mother said brightly, giving him one last hug.

"Spaghetti?" Michael asked, catching her enthusiasm.

"Spaghetti it is!" she answered, rising from beneath the oak tree and brushing her skirt. "And how about some ice cream for dessert?"

"Oh, yes," he said excitedly.

"Good. Why don't you help me set the table."

Together they left the lengthening shadows of the oak tree and started up the stairs. He thought of the game they played while doing the dishes. He didn't feel like playing that game tonight, but maybe tomorrow he'd start collecting happy moments for the prize of a shared candy bar.

The Home Front

At the start, he had to admit, the homecoming could not have been nicer. Everything he had pictured in his mind over and over again, until it seemed to have already occurred. Yet, when it finally did come, it seemed like a long-running play in which he had been miscast as the lead and didn't know his lines.

He had stepped off the plane and, squinting into the sun, spotted Joyce by her beautiful red hair, lush and gleaming, in the large crowd of shouting, waving, crying people waiting behind the airstrip's gate. Lugging all his gear, he had hurried towards her, seeing Joey, his nearly two-year-old son, standing solemnly in his mother's shadow. Someone opened the gate and the jubilant crowd surged forward.

A babble of joyous screams erupted as wives ran into their soldier-husbands' open arms and children of all ages danced excitedly around their entwined parents. Joyce had not rushed forward with the others but stood a little off to the side, holding Joey's hand and flashing that huge, toothy smile. God, how beautiful she is, he thought, as he reached her, dropped his gear and swept her up in his arms. He had almost forgotten how soft her body felt as he held her off the ground and drank in the fragrance of her neck and hair. For several seconds they said nothing, immutable in their first embrace. Then he heard her whisper, "Welcome home, Lieutenant," in that throaty voice he loved, and he found her lips and hungrily feasted on them.

Finally, he released her and turned his attention to his son who was gazing up at him with a quizzical stare. He bent down and swooped him up in his arms and saw an instant cloud of fear roll into the boy's eyes. Momentarily, a pang of disappointment seized him until he remembered that he had been away for eighteen months and Joey had been a four-month-old baby when he had left for Iraq.

"Hi, Joey," he said cheerfully, bouncing him lightly in his arms, but Joey continued his silent, confused stare. He let the boy down, and Joey immediately reached for his mother's hand and moved behind her.

"Give him a little time to get acquainted," Joyce said, offering a reassuring smile, and he nodded. "Come on! Everyone's waiting for you at home."

Home was the word that kept exploding in his brain. During his entire time in Iraq--all his missions, the ambushes, the fierce fighting, the deaths or mutilations of men in his platoon, the letters of condolence he laboriously composed to the relatives of the dead, the loneliness, the sexual frustration, the boredom of life back at camp-- brief relief came only from the arrival of mail from his parents and his brother and sister, but especially his wife.

He kept all her letters and when several days had gone by and he hadn't heard from her, he'd read some of her old letters, In the last several months of his tour, her letters were shorter and fewer, but he attributed this to her preoccupation with Joey who was almost two and, according to Joyce, was a very rambunctious kid. Still, he craved any news from home. *Home* was the symbolic word for love and safety and normalcy and life's renewal.

Last Christmas, when he heard the song, *There's No Place Like Home For The Holidays,* images of their modest, Cape Cod house flooded his brain as he pictured Joyce and Joey in their daily routines. Then he thought of his last Christmas at home and trimming the tree and exchanging gifts on Christmas Eve, because Joyce was too excited to wait any longer, and going to his parents' house for Christmas dinner. Invariably these daydreams led to the bedroom and reliving nights of lovemaking followed by sleeping pressed against her warm, pillowy body, and he ached for her.

Now, finally, after eighteen months of hell and endless, tormenting daydreams, he was home.

Lugging his heavy gear, he followed his wife to the car. His spirits had never been higher, yet the mere act of walking casually in the sunshine, devoid of fear and constant vigilance, without all his senses on alert, seemed somehow strange. He stowed his gear in the trunk and walked to the driver's side of the car to see that Joyce was already behind the wheel.

"I'll drive," he said, and she looked puzzled for a second and then jumped out and went around to the passenger's side.

"Sorry, Bob," she said with a half-smile as she took her seat beside him. "I'm just so used to driving."

"Sure, honey. Sure," he said, adjusting the driver's seat to accommodate his six-foot frame.

He realized that both of them felt awkward at that moment. They both had a lot of adjustments to make, which was only natural after being apart for so long, he reflected. They had only known each other for less than a year before they married, and Joey was conceived on their honeymoon and then four months after his birth, this long absence.

He glanced in the rear-view mirror at Joey placidly sitting in his car seat. He was a stranger to this child and would have to make up for lost time, to get to know this little boy, no longer a baby, his son. He silently vowed to make this a top priority.

On the hour's drive to their home, Joyce kept up most of the conversation, talking about neighbors and friends and telling him how every night before going to bed, Joey kissed his picture. "And I told him that today he could kiss his Daddy in person," she added cheerfully.

"Funny, he doesn't seem to relate my picture to me," was his half-jesting comment, with a tincture of disappointment.

"Because it's a small picture and you're a great big guy!" she reminded him. They both smiled.

They drove mostly in silence for the last half hour and he was grateful. His pounding headache was bad and he was eager to get home and take some pills. The pain was intense enough that his eyes were almost closing with each pulsation crashing against his temples. The headaches had started about a year ago while he was recovering from minor shrapnel wounds and a mild concussion in the Green Zone hospital. The doctors gave him a strong prescription and told him that they would soon stop. They didn't. Now he sensed they were a permanent legacy of his tour of duty.

He wished he didn't have to see people today; to just be with his wife and son, quiet and peaceful. He looked in the mirror at Joey, who had fallen asleep, and he wished he could do the same. Sleep was the one thing he craved almost as much as sex. Deep, deep sleep, undisturbed by nightmares and cold sweats and waking up to the sound of his fearful shouts. He had been living in a constant state of tiredness that sleeping pills and pep pills could not control.

As he drove down their block, he spotted the balloons first, a brilliant array of primary colors, floating aimlessly at the end of strings attached to their mailbox. He pulled into their driveway and the big, hand-painted sign, "Welcome Home Bob," anchored to the top of the garage, came into view, along with a crowd of people clustered in the small front yard.

Shouts and cheers and clapping now assaulted his ears, intensifying his headache, and he forced a smile. He knew most of the faces, even in their distorted hysteria, and he spotted his parents, his sister Gayle, his brother Russ and his best friend from high school, Steve Shelby, among the crowd.

As soon as he turned the engine off, everyone surrounded the car, banging excitedly on the hood and doors, echoing the bullets and mortar shells that telegraphed the sounds of death as a constant companion, triggering louder explosions in his head. He tried to smile as he exited the car.

A cacophony of greetings pierced his ears as women hugged him and men slapped him on the back. Then his mother was standing before him, her eyes overflowing with tears, her arms outstretched, and he nestled into them, fleetingly becoming a small boy again, relishing the safety and consolation of her embrace. She hugged him fiercely, protectively, and he thought of the mothers who would never hug their sons again. He closed his pain-seared eyes and was momentarily suspended in time and place. Then he felt another body pressing against his side and heard a familiar voice shouting in his ear, "Welcome home, son," and he extended one arm to include his father in this circle of comfort.

"Okay, Norma, don't hog the boy!" his father finally said in a parody of gruffness, gently disentangling his wife from his son. "Other people want to say hello."

His mother had no sooner let go of him when he was assaulted from front and back by his sister and brother, with another round of prolonged hugs. His headache seemed to intensify with each pat on his back and each greeting shouted in his ears. His best friend,

Steve Shelby, was pummeling his arm, shouting "You made it, buddy," but he could barely respond.

Finally, the crowd surged inside the house and out to the back yard, festooned with paper streamers, more balloons and another banner that he couldn't read because his vision was now blurred. He saw a long picnic table covered with platters of cold cuts and salads and breads and cookies. Neighbors who had deferred to his family in the driveway now surrounded him to offer individual greetings.

He tried to be polite, to focus on each person standing before him as they uttered sincerely meant platitudes. But he was acutely aware of the awkwardness that this current situation presented. Men who had never experienced war were attempting to establish a bond with him by expressing some intuitive understanding of what war was all about. From what they read or heard, they could imagine themselves vaingloriously in battles, and these fantasies bolstered their claims of kinship in knowing what he had been through.

He wanted to be kind but he felt nothing but contempt for their silly notions, as speakers salvaged their manly dignity by pretending to know what he must have endured. No imagining, no reading and no projecting could ever prepare one for the nightmarish realities of war. No one, except the men and women who had experienced the guts and terror of war, could claim an understanding of its everlasting impact on a human life. The gap between warriors and non-participants could never be bridged.

The warriors forever stood apart, locked in a brotherhood of searing images, torn psyches and barely repressed memories.

With the sun, the crowd and the noise, his pain had set his head on fire. Having greeted each guest with a clenched-teeth smile and a visible twitching at his temples, he retreated to the house for his pills. He hauled his gear up to the master bedroom, found his pills and quickly swallowed them without water. He staggered toward the bed and fell on it face-down.

The noise from the yard drifted up to him, and he covered his head with a pillow, for only silence and darkness could help relieve his torture. The pain dominated his consciousness and would not let go. He lay there grimacing at each wave of pain slapping against his skull, with barely a second of relief before the next pulsation. His intense suffering made time expand as seconds became minutes and minutes, hours. He had no idea when the pills took effect and he drifted off to sleep.

He awoke, totally disorientated, not knowing where he was and having no idea of how long he had slept. He realized the pain was gone. Then he saw Joyce sitting at the edge of the bed, staring at him with a look that at first seemed sullen but then he decided was just intense.

"How long have I been asleep?" he asked.

"About three hours," she said, breaking into a thin smile.

"Sorry," he said, returning her smile but feeling guilty.

"No problem," she said quickly. "I explained that you were exhausted after your flight, and everyone understood."

"Are they gone?"

"Yes, except for your Mom and Dad and your sister. They're helping me clean up. Your brother had to go to work."

He reached for her hand and drew her to him. He felt her body tighten. He cupped her face in his hands and kissed her, as pent-up desire and stored intimate images now consumed him. She briefly returned his kiss and then pulled away, laughing awkwardly as he held on to her arm.

"Your parents were hoping to say goodbye before they leave, and I should get back down to help them."

He was amazed how casually she said this, her whole demeanor reflecting coolness, in stark contrast to his white-hot ardent state.

"Why don't you grab a quick shower—you smell funky," she said with a forced giggle, "while I finish cleaning up." Still in the same casual tone, while rising from the bed, she said, "Then you can say goodbye to your Mom and Dad." She gave him a throw-away smile and headed for the door.

He lay on the bed in total confusion. The woman he had left eighteen months ago was as passionately eager in their lovemaking as he, but this was someone new, someone cool and remote. He felt that the postponement of any intimacy due to his parent's presence was a welcome excuse on her part rather than a reluctant obligation. What the hell was happening?

In acute confusion and frustration he rose from the bed and headed for the bathroom, stopping at the bureau for a fresh pair of civilian underwear. He opened the second drawer from the top, which was his underwear drawer, and found no shorts but Joyce's nightgowns. Losing focus, he rummaged through them and felt a sharp cardboard edge graze his finger. He grasped the object and pulled it out of the drawer. It was a picture within a cheap cardboard frame of Joyce and Steve Shelby, his high school buddy, and Joey. He studied it. He could tell it was a recent picture from Joey's appearance. It was a head shot of all three, like the pictures taken in the photo booths at amusement parks. Joyce and Steve's heads were leaning toward each other, actually touching, and Joey was propped up between them, holding a pinwheel. All three were smiling—no, laughing—happy and relaxed, conveying the casually intimate look of a young family.

He leaned against the bureau, still staring at the picture, struggling to respond to all its possible implications without drawing the one conclusion that he feared but which his mind kept racing toward. He didn't know how long he stood there, holding the picture, but he heard Joyce's voice floating behind him.

"I changed the drawers in case you were wondering where..." followed by silence.

Gripping the picture, he turned toward the voice, his mute accusation clearly visible in his eyes. Her eyes kept flicking between the picture and his face. He saw the color rushing from her cheeks. They stood motionless for several seconds while the air grew thick and hot.

"What's this all about?" he finally said.

She looked confused. Taking a few steps back, she sat on the bed, her head bent over as if she were studying the pattern of the carpet, her long hair shrouding her face.

He repeated his question, without moving from his spot. He saw her shoulders begin to tremble and he realized she was crying. He took a few steps toward her, pointing the picture at her face. He knew he was on the edge of an explosion more powerful than the sudden fits of anger he had experienced during the last year, and he thought briefly about the coping mechanisms—deep breathing, visualizations, even counting—that the army psychologist had recommended, but he dismissed them. His anxiety was too great.

"Goddammit it, Joyce, I want an answer!" he shouted in total frustration.

Without lifting her head, she spoke in a barely audible voice, interrupted with short sobs.

"I'm sorry. I was going to tell you but not on your first day home."

"Going to tell me what?" He decoded the answer from her whole demeanor, but his indignation demanded a pound of flesh: he wanted to hear her say it. He felt the first pulsations of another headache coming on.

"Steve and I...well...it was so hard for me, with you away... and Joey was such a handful... and I was so lonely."

She paused to wipe the tears from her face, but she never looked up at him.

"And?" was all he said as lights danced at the corners of his eyes and his temple swelled to accommodate the onrushing pain.

"And Steve was such a help and he...and he..." Her voice now came in one continuous wail. "I don't know how it happened. I didn't mean for it to happen." She broke off and buried her head in her hands.

There it was, right out there between them in plain sight, like some man-eating monster she had just vomited up to consume him. His mind raced riotously in random flashes. He felt ambushed, like those times in the war, and suddenly she was the enemy assaulting him, wanting to destroy him, and he had to protect himself.

The pain was exploding in his head again and his vision blurred her outline until she became a shapeless object of his blind hatred. He was back in Iraq, running on automatic pilot, sheer instinct and reactive fear. His adrenalin was pumping wildly.

He dropped the picture and, extending both arms, rushed toward her. He heard her scream once before his hands tightened around her throat and then he heard only gurgling sounds as her hands frantically clutched at his arms. The room was black. Nothing mattered but to destroy this thing that was trying to kill him.

Then he became aware of something grabbing at his legs as a small, wailing voice pierced his consciousness.

"Daddy, Daddy, Daddy," was the chant he vaguely heard echoing up to him as from some deep cavern far below him. A flicker of recognition brought him back to a hazy state of consciousness and he looked down and saw Joey's tear-stained face, a distorted mask of fear and anguish.

He released his grip and, sinking to his knees, clutched his son in a fierce bear hug. A sudden shift in the air current around him was the only indication that Joyce had left the bed and now, as he cradled Joey's bobbing head in his large hands, he saw her rush from the room.

Joey was now pushing against his chest and frantically calling, "Mommy! Mommy! Mommy!" He released the boy who ran after his mother. He leaned back against the side of the bed and, as full consciousness returned, considered with horror what had just taken place. Waves of massive pain crashed against his temples but could not blot out his repugnance for the scene he now relived. Confusion and hurt overwhelmed him. He was finding it hard to breathe.

"Bob, are you okay?" came the familiar voice of his father from the doorway, jolting him back from his concentrated misery. Before he could answer, his father was leaning over him, touching his shoulder and repeating "What's wrong, son?" in a tender tone that he had never heard before.

"What's wrong?" he repeated to himself, turning inward again. Just about every fucking thing in my life! I barely make it out of Iraq alive, to come home to find my wife's been screwing around with my best friend and my kid doesn't even know me. And these fucking headaches! And now I blacked out and almost killed my wife. Sweet Jesus, what's wrong? What's right would be a better question. Nothing!

He stared blankly at his father as tears welled in both men's eyes.

"I need help, Dad," was all he could muster, slumping to the floor.

"Yes, son, I see. We'll get you help."

He crawled over to his duffle bag and reached in for more pills, swallowing them hungrily without water. Pinpricks of light danced before his eyes and he couldn't rise up on his legs. He crawled back to the bed and rested his pain-racked head against the cool satin coverlet.

Downstairs he could hear his parents' voices and his sister's, all talking over each other in high, agitated tones. Then he heard his father say, "Hello. This is an emergency. It's my son. He just returned from Iraq."

The talking downstairs continued but he blotted it out. He closed his eyes and now the dancing lights were kaleidoscopic, bouncing around his eyeballs like rushing atoms. His breathing was still shallow and his body was soaked with sweat.

He met the pulsating pain and went into it, lost in a crazy patchwork of jumbled scenes where death and fear, love and hope, destruction and despair carried him off to nether regions he had never wished to explore. This living nightmare was now his warrior's legacy from which he could find no peace.

Then he felt a body kneeling by his side as strong arms encircled his shoulders. "Help is on the way, son," his father said in a strong, reassuring voice. 'Help is on the way."

He leaned into his father, sinking down in the warmth of his comforting embrace, and felt his breathing slow. The pain didn't seem quite so intolerable any more.

Hands

On the first day of kindergarten Patricia Healy met Alison Scotto when they sat next to each other for mid- morning snack. At noontime, when the two girls emerged from school at the end of the half-day class, they approached their nervously waiting mothers and, holding hands, announced that they were now best friends.

"That's nice," Mrs. Healy said, exchanging a bemused smile with Mrs. Scotto, relieved that her daughter had had a good first-day experience.

"What's your friend's name?" Mrs. Scotto asked solicitously with a tilt of her head. Before Alison could answer, Patricia spoke up. "Patti," she said, with both assurance and assertiveness in her voice. Turning to her mother, she said, "Mommy, this is Alison."

"Hello, Alison," Mrs. Healy said, extending her hand to the child, who shyly reached for it.

"Alison Scotto," Mrs. Scotto added.

"We're the Healy family," Mrs. Healy said, shifting her extended hand to Alison's mother.

"Nice to meet you," Mrs. Scotto said.

"Mommy," Patti spoke up boldly, "you promised to take me to The Windmill for lunch. Can Alison come too?"

Caught off guard, Mrs. Healy hedged. "I don't know, dear. Perhaps Mrs. Scotto has other plans for lunch."

Mrs. Scotto gave Mrs. Healy a half smile and in a tentative voice said, "Actually we don't"

Mrs. Healy felt a twinge of annoyance. She had wanted a private mother-daughter lunch with Patti, celebrating this special day. Now she'd have to make small talk with a perfect stranger, and the mother seemed as shy as the daughter.

"Patti loves The Windmill because they have a separate children's menu," Mrs. Healy explained. "Would you like to join us?"

"Yes," said Mrs. Scotto, who paused before adding, "If you don't mind."

Mrs. Healy caught the bright smiles of both children and, dismissing any petty annoyance, said enthusiastically, "Then it's settled. Off we go!"

Each girl instinctively took her mother's hand without releasing each other's grip, so they walked in a straight horizontal line toward the parking area.

"Why don't we all go in my van and I'll drop you off back here," Mrs. Healy suggested.

"Just let me grab my bag," Mrs. Scotto said before breaking ranks with the other three and hurrying toward her car. Mrs. Healy noted that it was a battered, old sedan.

"Here we are!" Mrs. Healy said, stopping by the side of a shiny Lexus SUV.

"This is beautiful!" Mrs. Scotto exclaimed in a genuine tone of wonderment as the mothers settled into the front seats.

"Everyone buckled up?" Mrs. Healy asked, surveying the two giggling girls in the next row of seats and thinking that the physical contrast between the two could not be more startling.

While Patti Healy was tall for her age and thin as a string bean, with reddish-blond hair and freckles dotting a face that, all her relatives agreed, had the map of Ireland on it, Alison was short, plump, olive-skinned and, with dark eyes and heavy brows and lashes, exotic looking.

Patti, always a leader, was helping Alison with her seat belt. Once this task was completed, they remained holding hands, clearly enjoying the novelty of their newly found friendship.

The fifteen-minute drive to The Windmill was spent in two distinct conversations. In the rear seat Patti told Alison about her family's summer trip to Disney World, with Alison mostly playing an appreciative audience for all the marvels Patti described. From the questions Alison asked, it was clear to Mrs. Healy that the Scotto family had not yet made this trip.

In the front seat, Mrs. Healy was making chit-chat while politely probing Mrs. Scotto for the usual information acceptable when two people are suddenly thrust together under unexpected, tenuous circumstances; yet, in that typically American fashion, the questions could be considered remarkably personal. By the time they arrived at The Windmill, the two women had exchanged information sufficient to form the broadest outline of their current lives.

Mrs. Healy, newly introduced as Janet, imparted that her husband, Ned, was a lawyer in private practice, specializing in taxes, wills and estates; Patti was their only child—she had had two miscarriages before Patti was born and one after--and her doctor had "put his foot down and that was the end of that." Both she and Ned were natives to their town and had met in high school, separated for four years while she pursued a nursing degree and he got his bachelor's. Reunited shortly after his college graduation, they married right after he received his law degree "and passed the bar exam." She had retired from nursing on Patti's arrival.

As for Mrs. Scotto, now Helena, she was new to the community, having arrived only a month earlier when her husband, a master sergeant—career army and newly returned from his second duty tour in Iraq—was stationed at the nearby army base as a firearms instructor. Alison was their only child.

"We put off having any more children until Joe was back home," she explained. Then she added a puzzling remark, "Now I'm not so sure," in a strangely wistful tone, before changing the subject.

Janet felt it would be inappropriate to ask a follow-up question.

At The Windmill the party of four was quickly seated in a booth and Patti took charge of describing to Alison the best dishes on the children's menu. Aware of her daughter's strong personality, Janet noted that Alison seemed perfectly content, even happy, to let Patti take the lead.

After the waitress came and took their orders, the two mothers listened as Patti, with a few additions from Alison, described the events of the morning with much enthusiasm. When that topic ended, Patti started telling Alison about her doll collection. An awkward moment ensued as the mothers, virtual strangers, faced each other across the table. Finally, Janet said, "So how do you like our town?"

Helena responded with another tentative smile. "We're still getting settled in. We rented a little house that was cheap but is a real fixer-upper, so we've been busy making it livable."

Janet nodded appreciatively.

"Our neighbors don't seem very friendly," Helena added, casting her eyes down at the table.

Aware of the town's social complexities, Janet knew the prejudices of the blue-collar "townies" against the transient army families. "Give them time," she said with an encouraging smile. "They'll warm up to you."

"I hope so," Helena said with a rueful look washing over her face. Momentarily she appeared on the verge of tears. Janet felt embarrassed that they had unexpectedly stumbled into an area that was clearly troubling to Helena, so she switched her attention back to the girls.

"How are the hamburgers?" she asked brightly. Both girls shook their heads in vigorous approval. Hoping to keep the conversation light, she turned back to Helena.

"Patti is such a picky eater! I can't get her to eat many vegetables, but she has a real sweet tooth."

Helena nodded. "Alison is the same way. Now that Joe is home, he insists that she eat her vegetables or she doesn't get any dessert." She paused and again looked down at the table. "Our dinners have become a real battle ground...a test of wills. I dread them."

Janet was now annoyed. No matter what she said, it seemed to trigger some disturbing response in this woman she had just met under the most casual circumstances. She had already assessed the situation and determined that there would be no social connection, so she was indignant at being dragged into a deep vein of personal issues with this stranger.

"They make such great salads here!" she said quickly and spent the next several minutes silently consuming her greens.

"Mommy, can Alison and I go watch the fish?" Patti asked, having finished her cheeseburger and fries. Patti was referring to the large fish tank filled with vividly colored tropical fish in the lobby of The Windmill.

"Yes, dear, but don't get in anyone's way," Janet said. "We'll be there in a minute."

Patti and Alison left the booth and the two mothers watched them walking hand in hand toward the fish tank.

"I guess we're finished too," Janet said with too bright a smile, looking for the waitress, "unless you want some coffee."

"Yes, please," Helena said and Janet was annoyed again that this brief but awkward encounter could not be quickly ended. The waitress appeared. "Two coffees and the check, please," Janet said tersely.

"You know, you're the first person I've said more than ten words to, since moving here," Helena confessed in a tone that Janet found much too intimate. "It's good to have someone to talk to," Helena said shyly.

Janet grew more uncomfortable and angry and made no reply, looking for the waitress with the coffee. When it came, she busied herself with pouring milk and sugar and stirring it vigorously. She started taking unusually large gulps in hopes of ending this meeting, but Helena continued to stir her coffee rhythmically in an abstracted manner without touching it.

Finally Helena put her spoon down and looked directly at Janet as her whole face seemed to crumple and she spoke in a low, hesitant voice.

"Joe's been away for so long—nearly three years on his two tours—that I didn't realize how much everything would change when he came home."

Totally disconcerted by Helena's confession, Janet focused her attention on the check, calculating the tip, hoping her action would discourage any further revelations.

Helena continued in a tone that sounded as if she were talking to herself. "Joe wants to be the man of the house and I can understand that, but I've been on my own with Alison for so long, taking care of things, I just can't go back to what I was when we were first married. We're arguing all the time. He doesn't seem to understand that we're both different people for all the things we've been through. Sometimes I feel I can't breathe." She paused and now, with a distinct tremble in her voice asked, "Am I making any sense?"

Janet looked up from the check and saw Helena's eyes beginning to mist. Not wishing to be sucked any further into this emotional vortex, she offered a half-smile. "It's a difficult period of adjustment but I'm sure you'll work it out," she said crisply, as though this were a trifling matter undeserving of any more discussion. Now she busied herself rummaging through her bag, finding her wallet and extracting a credit card.

"How much do I owe?" Helena asked in a tremulous voice. Janet looked at her and saw the tears dotting her cheeks.

"This is my treat," she said.

"Then it's mine the next time," Helena responded quickly.

"Sure!" Janet said abstractly, motioning for the waitress who was hovering nearby, aborting any additional exchanges.

They sat in silence, Janet avoiding any eye contact, for the interminable time it took the waitress to return. Finally, Helena, dabbing at her eyes with a tissue, said, "I'm sorry. I shouldn't be pouring my troubles out to you. It's just that..."

Janet interrupted her with a curt "I understand," while continuing to look for the returning waitress, a clear expression of impatience shadowing her face. Helena said nothing more. The waitress having finally returned, Janet quickly scribbled the tip and her signature and rose from the booth. She walked briskly toward the entrance, Helena following behind her.

From a distance the two women could see their daughters still holding hands, gazing at the brightly colored fish swimming languorously in the large fish tank.

"Oh, Mommy, they're so beautiful!" Patti exclaimed, spotting her mother's approach.

"Yes, dear," Janet responded, taking her daughter's hand. Patti was still holding Alison's hand.

"Can Alison come home with us and see my turtle?" Patti asked in a self-assured tone that was precocious for a five-year-old. Alison was looking at Janet with big dark-brown eyes, swimming with questions.

"Not today, dear," Janet said, not unkindly. "Mommy has a lot of errands to run."

"Tomorrow?" Patti asked tenaciously.

"We'll see," Janet said with an unusual note of exasperation that the bright, sensitive Patti caught in her mother's voice and fell into confused silence.

The ride back to the school parking lot seemed multiple times as long as the ride to The Windmill. Both mothers silently listened to their daughters' prattle. For once, Alison was the main speaker, telling Patti about the different places they had lived. Patti, who had never know any home but the large brick house she had been raised in, listened attentively as Alison described a trailer, an apartment and a farmhouse where her grandparents lived.

Patti could never be silent for long. Now she was telling Alison about her ballet lessons and piano lessons and gymnastics class. In answer to Patti's question about what lessons Alison took, she answered, "My Mom is teaching me how to cook." Patti gave a little laugh but, reading Alison's confused expression, said, "That's nice."

Thinking how vastly different was the background of these two girls, Janet stole a sideways glance at Helena who was staring straight ahead, her eyes still moist, her mouth set in a determined lock. Finally, they reached the school parking lot and Janet pulled up to Helena's old sedan.

"We'll see you in school tomorrow," Janet said to Alison.

"Mom," Alison said in a small voice, "can Patti come to visit us after school tomorrow?"

In a cold, flat voice her mother answered, "That's up to Mrs. Healy and I'm sure she's very busy."

Janet gave Helena an embarrassed, shallow smile. "We'll see," was her vague response that all three passengers seemed to understand as brooking no further discussion. To break the eerie silence that followed her answer, Janet assumed her public cheery voice.

"It was nice to meet you," she said as Helena opened her door and slid out of the Lexus.

"Yeah," was all she said in reply. Then she turned to help Alison out of the SUV and added, "Thanks for lunch."

"My pleasure," Janet chirped in an airy tone so light it could be carried on the wind.

Patti scrambled over to the seat just vacated by Alison and called to her. "See you tomorrow, Alison. Remember we're best friends."

"Buckle up, dear," Janet said distractedly.

As the Lexus pulled away, Patti and Alison waved to each other. The distance between the two vehicles grew greater with each second but Janet could see in the rear-view mirror Patti's hand still frantically waving. Janet was already planning the delicate discussion she'd have with Patti over milk and home-made cookies later that afternoon.

Ruth And Naomi

Rigid with anticipation, Naomi Rogers stood in the airline terminal, her nose practically pressed against the huge glass window, watching the disembarking passengers. Finally, when the line of people descending the steps had slowed to a trickle, she spotted her. Ruth stood at the top of the stairs, pausing to adjust the strap of a large shoulder bag before reaching for the handrail. Firmly holding the baby with one arm, she started her cautious descent.

With an intense focus Naomi watched the tall, young woman, her short ash-blond hair gleaming in the sunlight, taking long, graceful strides across the tarmac. The baby, invisible beneath a blanket and hat, was a small lump pressed against his mother's chest. Stephen Paterson Rogers Jr., Steve's son, her grandson, the only one she would ever have. Misery swept across Naomi's face like a storm cloud whipped across the horizon by a strong wind, but she recomposed her expression, banishing sad thoughts as her daughter-in law entered the terminal and she rushed forward to meet her.

"Welcome, welcome!" she fairly shouted in an effort to be normal and wrapped her arms around Ruth, careful not to squash the baby.

Naomi avoided looking at Ruth directly, fearful that the forlorn gaze in the young woman's eyes would match her pathetic attempt to mask her own fathomless sadness. Still entwined, a small private circle of unexpressed grief, the two women did a sideways shuffle away from the door.

"Here's your grandson," Ruth said laconically as she pulled the blanket back to reveal the two-month-old baby. Naomi gazed at the placid sleeping face, the small mouth puckered in sucking motions. She touched a tiny hand that reflexively grasped her finger and held on to it. The baby's eyes opened and gave Naomi an unfocused stare before closing again, but in that brief moment Naomi saw the blue reflection of her son. A new wave of sadness washed over her.

Quickly she grabbed Ruth's arm. "Let's get your luggage and get you home. You must be tired after so long a trip."

For Naomi, the rules of the game for this first meeting between the two women under these extraordinary circumstances were simple: immerse yourself in ordinary conversation about everyday, inconsequential things, even the silliest small talk, avoiding silences that could open chasms of mutual grief.

On the forty-minute drive to Naomi's house, both women were playing the game well; still, there were awkward gaps filled with silence but, Naomi reasoned, that was to be expected. After all, she and Ruth were almost strangers whose only connection was a dead son and husband and now this baby, Steve's living legacy.

Shortly after leaving the airport, the baby had started crying and Ruth nursed him. The tentative conversation centered mostly on the baby, as each woman avoided entering the personal space of the other, fearful of plunging into unchartered depths.

"Here we are!" Naomi said, pulling into the driveway of a modest ranch house with a small manicured front lawn sporting one shade tree. As they entered the house, Naomi realized that the terms of this visit, except to attend Steve's burial in the family plot, were undefined.

"I'm so glad you're here, Ruth," she said—and meant it. "I got Steve's crib down from the attic for the baby."

She led Ruth through the small living room to the guest room where she set Ruth's suitcase on the window seat. Ruth walked over to the crib and hesitated for just a moment, seeming lost in thought, before laying the baby, sleeping again, in the crib.

The two women stood side by side gazing down at the serene infant. Naomi wondered if Ruth had the same thought as she, that this child was lying exactly where his father had lain as a baby. But this small, proud token of family continuity quickly steered both women to hellish reminders of Steve's absence.

Ruth's shoulders began to tremble and she backed away from the crib and sat on the bed, her hands hiding her face. Naomi sat beside her and, saying nothing, patted Ruth's shoulder.

Unexpectedly, Ruth erupted with a prolonged sob and buried her head against Naomi's chest.

"I miss him! I miss him so much!" she wailed, struggling between sobs to speak.

Naomi cradled Ruth's shaking head, gently stroking her hair, rocking her back and forth. "I know, I know," she said again and again as her own eyes welled with tears.

Finally, Ruth straightened up, wiping her eyes with the back of her hands. She spoke softly. "We had such plans. When he got home from Iraq he was going to finish college and become a teacher."

"Like his father, God rest his soul," Naomi inserted proudly, realizing suddenly that there were now two souls to pray for.

"He was so happy about the baby. He sent letters to him. I brought them for you to see. All about the dreams and hopes he had for his son. And all the things he looked forward to doing with him and with the three of us as a family." Ruth paused as fresh tears splashed across her cheeks. "All gone! All gone!" she said, her voice a small, anguished cry.

Naomi sensed that Ruth seemed on the verge of a meltdown. "You've had a long trip and must be tired. Why don't you lie down for a while and get some rest?" she suggested.

Dazedly, Ruth agreed and lay across the bed. Naomi closed the blinds and shut the door to the darkened room. She walked robotic-like to the living room and collapsed into a chair, all color draining from her face.

In the two weeks since news of Steve's death had reached her, she had denied herself a deep, purging grief. She lived day to day with the fact of his death like some nasty stranger invading her home, tempting her to rage and despair, luring her into dark recesses of her mind where she feared she could be lost forever. So she resisted, fought, would not surrender, and kept everything at a distance.

Her only child was dead. Each morning upon waking, this was her first thought of the day, but rather than dwell on it and plunge headlong into a vast sinkhole of hopelessness, she pushed it away, refusing to explore it throughout the day. Mundane chores that she had performed on auto-pilot before, like preparing her meals, making her bed and cleaning her home, she now gave intense concentration to, attempting to shut out all stray, dark thoughts. It was the only way she knew how to cope and survive.

Those errant thoughts that involuntarily, brazenly popped out when least expected dealt with memories of Steve as a baby, a boy, a teenager, a young man, up to his twenty-second birthday, his last. When she cleaned his room or glanced at his framed picture in uniform as she passed through the living room or saw his old, rusted bicycle still stored in a corner of the garage, at those moments he jumped vividly to life and her titanic battle to suppress haunting memories would be waged once again.

But now with Ruth's arrival and the baby, the new dimension of Steve's denied future was suddenly searing her brain, exciting her to great temptations of jet-black distress.

Summoning all her resources to fight against these disconsolate feelings, she thought of the beautiful baby sleeping peacefully in her guest room and the pretty young woman whom Steve had chosen as his wife. Then another thought came to her: in helping Ruth to cope with her loss, Naomi might deflect her own whirlpool of grief.

She realized how little she knew about Ruth. An excited call from Steve on the eve of his shipping out to Iraq, announcing his impromptu wedding that morning, two thousand miles away from home, was the first time she had heard Ruth's name or exchanged casual pleasantries with her when Steve put her on the phone.

She recalled how Ruth had said she was sorry Naomi lived so far away that it wasn't possible for her to attend the hastily-decided wedding, especially since the bride had no family and it would have been nice to have one relative in attendance.

Subsequent letters from Steve mentioned how pretty Ruth was, how smart, how sweet and how much he loved her. To Naomi's inquiries on more substantive facts about Ruth, Steve replied that she was twenty four—two years older than Steve so, he joked, he could really call her his old lady—she had been raised in foster homes, now worked as a sales clerk in a department store and shared an apartment with two other girls from the same store.

A few weeks after Steve's arrival in Iraq, Naomi received a call from Ruth.

"I know you live alone and I'm sure you're missing Steve and I hope you don't mind my calling you from time to time," Ruth said in a cheerful but tentative voice, suggesting an innate shyness.

"I'm delighted you called," Naomi said with genuine glee. "I wanted to call you but I know you're a busy working girl and have two roommates and I didn't want to bother anyone."

"Yes, it's better if I call you," Ruth said.

"Then call me anytime. Anytime at all," Naomi said. She paused and chuckled. "You're my only daughter-in law."

"Yes, swell!" came Ruth's happy response, and then they chatted some more about the meager information Steve shared with either of them on his life in Iraq.

"He doesn't say much about that," Ruth confessed. "He talks mostly about the future."

Still, what little they could glean from Steve's incidental remarks, they shared. Ruth's calls came regularly about every two weeks and Naomi looked forward to them.

Shyly, Ruth began asking Naomi about Steve's father who had died of a heart attack when Steve was twelve. Naomi was happy to share her memories, and through this sharing both women seemed to draw closer to Steve's living presence.

"It must have been so hard for you," Ruth exclaimed at one point. "Did you ever think of remarrying?"

"Yes," Naomi confessed. "I was forty-four when Frank died, and after a while a few men asked me out. But nothing really clicked and I had my job and Steve."

Naomi asked Ruth about being in foster care.

"It was okay," she responded in a flat tone, "but I always felt like an outsider. Like nobody really cared about me..." There was a pause and her voice brightened, "Until I met Steve."

Naomi liked this shy, honest girl, and through their phone conversations she felt a tenuous bond. Then came Ruth's excited call saying she was pregnant. Naomi greeted this news with conflicted feelings: joy that her only child was giving her a grandchild; concern that they were so young and unsettled to be starting a family. To Ruth she expressed great delight.

Ruth quit her job in her eighth month. Naomi thought about flying east to North Carolina to be with Ruth when the baby was due, but, as she explained to Ruth, she worked in a non-union office and couldn't take the time off without jeopardizing her job.

Ruth was cheerfully reassuring. "That's okay. My two roommates are almost as excited about the baby as I am. They take good care of me."

Late one night, a phone call from Nancy, one of Ruth's roommates. "Congratulations, Grandma! You have a healthy grandson, six pounds, ten ounces. Both mother and son are doing fine." Followed shortly by an excited Steve, calling from Iraq. "Isn't it great, Mom? A son! A grandson! I can't wait to see him!"

Pictures of Ruth and the baby were regularly received, and the obvious joy of her son and daughter-in-law banished any misgivings Naomi harbored. Ruth's phone calls increased to at least once each week, with the latest details of the baby's sleeping, eating, pooping, gurgling and growing trends.

"I'm having the baby christened next month," Ruth announced on one of her calls, with her usual excitement, "and I'm thinking of naming him after his father. What do you think?"

Silent for a moment as her heart did a thumping dance, Naomi finally said, "I think that's a wonderful idea."

"Good! I hoped you'd say that. Steve's thrilled. Then it's settled. But no one can call him Junior!"

"Agreed," Naomi said. Both women laughed.

By the next phone call the world had rocketed out of its orbit and been hurled into a timeless, bottomless black hole. Steve was gone, the victim of a sniper's bullet while on patrol. Naomi listened to Ruth's bottomless sobs while steeling herself to be strong for her daughter-in-law. After the initial purgative call, an unstated pact arose in which the two women focused their exchanges on the baby. The living sheltered the dead.

Now Ruth and the baby were here and tomorrow would be a rock-hard day, given over to the solemn rituals of burying a fallen soldier. Naomi thought of the news programs she had watched, highlighting the scandalously neglectful treatment of wounded veterans. She had fought to dispel fleeting images of Steve returning in a wheelchair, missing legs or an arm, but she never allowed herself to think of his being gone. The finality of that fact, she realized, would be hammered home tomorrow when he was lowered into the ground.

The baby would have nothing in the future to remind him of his father except pictures and a precisely folded flag. Then Naomi thought of the letters Ruth said Steve had written to his son, and she wondered if Steve had had a presentiment of his death or did every soldier live with the shadow of death as a casual friend. She was eager to read those letters, to catch a glimpse of the final transformation of her son—the full man he had become.

Naomi closed her eyes, desperate to escape from the burdens of her thoughts, and she must have dozed off. She was awakened by the sound of a door opening and saw Ruth coming toward her. Instantly she jumped back into sharp focus.

"My goodness, I must get dinner started," she said, rising from her chair. "You must be hungry."

"No rush," Ruth said, a half-smile deepening the lines of weariness around her eyes. "Let me help."

The two women moved into the kitchen.

"How does pork chops, rice, carrots and a salad sound?" Naomi asked, opening the refrigerator door.

"Delicious!" Ruth replied distractedly, her focus clearly not on food.

"Why don't you peel the carrots while I get the water boiling for the rice and start the salad," Naomi suggested, extracting lettuce, tomatoes and carrots from the vegetable bin.

Ruth nodded her agreement.

The women worked mostly in silence as they advanced through the preparation of the meal, but Naomi found a tremendous comfort in Ruth's presence. This is the woman that Steve loved, she thought, and his baby is sleeping in the same room where his father slept as a baby. Occasionally, she'd glance at Ruth and catch the young woman returning her look. Awkwardly they'd both smile, and Naomi wondered if Ruth was deriving as much comfort as she.

"Let's eat in the dining room," Naomi suggested, "and have candles." She paused. "To welcome you and the baby."

Seated at the small round dining room table, they ate silently, the flickering candlelight distorting the small smiles they exchanged. But Naomi did not feel awkward; she felt peaceful. Thoughts were forming in her mind that, as yet, she could not speak.

"This cake is delicious," Ruth said, summoning some of her old cheery tones, as Naomi sipped her coffee.

"Pineapple upside-down cake is my one specialty. It's my mother's recipe," Naomi said, her own voice brightening.

"It's nice to have family traditions," Ruth said in a wistful tone, and Naomi, igniting with pity, wanted to rush to Ruth and embrace her. Fearful of the floodgates such an action might open, she swallowed hard, took another sip of coffee and said, "What are your plans now?"

"I don't really know. I haven't had time to think about the future." She seemed confused and on the verge of tears.

"Do you have many ties back east?" Naomi asked gently.

"Not really," Ruth said, gazing absently at the table. "My job. A few friends." Then, as an afterthought, "I have to find a new apartment. Our place is too crowded with the baby. My roommates are sweet but..." Her voice trailed off.

Naomi saw her opening and her words tumbled out. "Ruth, would you consider moving to Oregon and living here with me? There's plenty of room and you could get a sales job here and I could help with little Steve" It was the first time Naomi had called the baby "little Steve," and she felt momentarily happy, reassured, with the sound of it.

Ruth's eyes shot up to look directly at Naomi. "Do you really mean it?"

Naomi reached across the table and squeezed Ruth's hand. "Of course, I mean it! I'm alone and you're alone and you're going to need help with the baby. Why shouldn't we be together? We're family."

"Family," Ruth repeated the work like an incantation. "That would be nice."

Not wishing to pressure Ruth, Naomi said brightly, "Think about it," as she rose to clear the table. She carried the dessert dishes into the kitchen and began rinsing them. Ruth followed her and silently began stacking the rinsed dishes in the dishwasher. When the last dish was stacked, the dishwasher door closed, and the dials set, the two women found themselves standing face to face.

"I would love to come and live with you," Ruth said quietly, "and be a family."

Naomi hugged Ruth. They heard the baby crying in the bedroom and they both smiled conspiratorially, fully at ease now, confirmed in their mutual love for souls new and departed.

Deep Waters

When he arrives at the beach, there are only a few people in the water, mostly old people wading in the shallows, wearing those funny hats-- baseball caps or straw hats with floppy brims--that old people like to wear. The beach is usually quiet during the week and he easily finds a deserted area.

Quickly he sets his towel on the sand, anchoring it with his military boots, and strips down to his bathing suit. As he wades into the warm Caribbean water, he waves to the old folks off to the side and they smile and wave back. This casual, spontaneous greeting is typical for people in Puerto Rico, whether natives, like him, or visitors adjusting to the relaxed, friendly atmosphere.

He dives below the small waves and with strong strokes swims out past the curling surf into the calm, deep water. When he finally stops swimming, he notices for the first time a man's head bobbing a short distance away from him, white hair fringing a bald dome. He's surprised to see an old man this far out from shore. The old man is smiling at him.

"You're a strong swimmer!" the old man says, spurting water from his mouth.

"Yes, sir!" he answers cheerfully. "Been swimmin' all my life. My father teach me when I was a baby."

"Is that so," the old man says with another smile distorted by the water bubbling around his face as his arms wave up and down just below the surface in a slow dog paddle. "It's a beautiful day," he adds, tilting his head up to survey the cloudless sky.

The young man laughs. "Most days in Puerto Rico are beautiful!"

"I know," the old man quickly responds. "That's why I come here every year from Vermont to escape our winters. Are you a native?"

"Yes, sir. I come from Mayaguez, just up the coast. I'm home on leave."

"Oh, you're in the army?"

"No, sir, the Marines," the young man says with unabashed pride. "Just got back from Iraq. Can't wait to get back."

The old man now has a quizzical look on his face.

"Get back?"

"Yes, sir, for my second tour of duty. I miss my buddies. The guys in my platoon, we're all really tight. They're my best friends. We cover each other." The young man pauses and then asks, "Were you in the service? I mean, when you were young."

The old man quietly says "Yes."

"Did you see any action?"

There's a pause before the old man answers. "Quite a bit." He offers no details and something in his look and the tone of his voice stops the young man from pursuing this topic.

"Two of my platoon buddies got injured and another guy got killed," the young man says, shifting the focus to his combat experience. "I got grazed on the shoulder—only a scratch." He smiles, pleased with this history.

"And you still want to go back to Iraq?" the old man asks, with a hint of condescension.

"Yes, sir, I sure do," the young man answers emphatically. "We've got to stop the terrorists from hitting us again."

"And you're fighting terrorists in Iraq, are you?" the old man asks. "You're fighting Al Qaeda?"

"That's what the president says," the young man replies, exuberant conviction in his voice. "And he's my commander-in-chief and what he says, goes."

"So you're fighting for something you believe in, then?" the old man asks kindly, an enigmatic smile forming on his water-splashed face.

The young man pauses, struggling to form an answer to so broad a question.

"I believe in the Marines," he says finally, his voice flushed with conviction. "I'm proud to wear the uniform and the respect it gets. My Marine buddies cover my back and I cover theirs. We've been through a lot together. Before I joined the Marines, I was pretty messed up and now I've got a career and I'm proud to be fighting for my country and democracy." The young man flashes a broad smile, displaying strong white teeth, pleased with his answer.

"I see," the old man says quietly, as his smile slowly fades into a weary expression.

"You didn't say what branch of the service you were in" says the young man.

"Oh, I was army," the old man replies. "Korea." Again, a look comes into his eyes that tells the young man this topic is closed. "Can I ask how old you are?"

"I'm nineteen."

"Nineteen," the old man says in a far-off voice. "With your whole life ahead of you."

The young man flashes another big smile. "Yes, sir."

"All Marine to the core, huh?" the old man says. "*Semper fidelis* and all that. right?"

"Yes, sir, absolutely."

The old man shifts his gaze to the open waters and seems to be in deep thought. The young man looks to the shore and sees a lady in a white beach robe and a floppy hat waving both her arms in their direction.

"I think that lady is trying to get your attention, sir," he says, and the old man says "What?" and turns his gaze toward the shore. "Oh, that's my wife. It must be time for lunch. Well, it's been nice talking with you. Good luck on your next tour."

The old man starts heading toward the shore with a slow dog-paddle and the young man marvels that he was able to swim this far out using such a slow stroke. When the old man is about twenty feet away from him, he suddenly turns and says "God keep you, Marine," in an unsteady voice.

The young man watches his slow bobbing progress until he finally reaches the shallows. His wife wades in and seems to be assisting him to stand. As the old man's body emerges from the gently lapping waves, the young man sees that he is missing his entire right leg. Leaning on his wife, they make their way slowly across the sand and finally disappear behind the gate of the condo complex that abuts the beach.

The young man is full of questions as unsettling thoughts crowd into his brain like dark rain clouds racing across a brilliant sun. Shaking his head as if to dismiss them, he turns toward the open water and with powerful strokes swims confidently away from the safety of the shore.

April Updates

Among the street people of Seattle news traveled fast. There were two distinct homeless communities within the city: the young drifters, naive and temporarily rebellious, herding together for protection and comfort; and the older, confirmed denizens of alleys, parks and soup kitchens. Within this latter group a loosely-knit confederacy had formed, primarily for sharing information vital for survival. What churches were serving food or distributing clothing; what areas had come under police surveillance; and what members of the brotherhood had been hassled or attacked.

Scott Matthews had been a recognized member of the confederation for nearly three years and went by the moniker of Bullet, so named by the other street people, and accepted by him, for his hair-trigger temper and the lightning speed with which he moved against anyone who bothered, annoyed or provoked him. Compact and wiry, it was not his physical size that intimidated others as much as a ferocious intensity and a menacing stare that conveyed a capacity for unstoppable rage bordering on insanity.

Bullet was an appropriate name for a second reason. He was known to have taken a bullet in his head while on patrol as a soldier in Iraq—a bullet that had not been removed for fear of massive brain damage but which added to the intense aura that surrounded him. Bullet spoke little when men gathered for free meals and he had never been seen in a shelter.

Among the street people there were several older men who had served in other wars and with them Bullet was a loyal, if distant, comrade, willing to help out a fellow veteran with a buck or aid him in getting medical attention or a safe place to crash. Still, he kept mostly to himself.

Old Mac, a Korean veteran, saw Bullet sunning himself in a downtown park on an early April morning and quickly made his way to Bullet's side. If anyone could claim a friendship with Bullet, it was Old Mac. On the third day of Bullet's arrival in Seattle, he had met the old man in this very park. It was one of the rare days when Old Mac was sober, not from any resolution to be sober but from a lack of money to buy his favorite cheap booze.

After brief introductions and some casual conversation, Bullet had treated Old Mac to breakfast and, seeing the old man's shakes, given him money for a pint. Such kindness was not lost on Old Mac who repaid the young man's generosity by serving as his guide--once he had imbibed enough to feel human again--to all the byways and protocols of the sprawling city.

For the next week they had even slept in an abandoned building that Old Mac knew to be safe, and the old man had steered his young protégé to the best places for free food, clothing, panhandling and bottle collecting. In the course of their wanderings, Old Mac talked about his experience in Korea. Bullet, however, was silent about his time in Iraq except to acknowledge that he had seen a lot of action there and to joke about the bullet in his head that couldn't be extracted, so he'd posed a challenge to the security guards at the airport metal detectors.

Unlike Old Mac, Bullet didn't drink and he wasn't interested in panhandling. The old man quickly sensed the brooding, forbidding aspects of this young veteran's personality and his preference for spending most of his time alone. After their first week together Bullet had moved on, but whenever they met up thereafter, they both seemed pleased with the encounter. Then one incident occurred that cemented their relationship forever and caused Old Mac to feel actual affection for his friend. It also brought Scott Matthews his new street name of Bullet.

Having drunk himself into a stupor, Old Mac had let down his guard and was sleeping in the doorway of a shuttered store in plain view of passersby. A trio of young street punks came upon him lying there.

"Look at this old dirt bag," one of them exclaimed as all three stood over the sleeping, snoring figure. "Let's see if he has any money."

Ignoring the strong, sour smell –"Christ, he stinks!"–one punk quickly rifled through the pockets of Old Mac's filthy pants. Finding nothing seemed to infuriate him.

"This piece of shit doesn't deserve to live!" he said, straightening up. The others nodded in agreement. Simultaneously, all three began kicking the snoring body in a frenzy of loathing, arousing Old Mac from his deep sleep. Instantly alarmed, he gazed up at the three young faces and saw the looks of rage.

"What the hell..." he yelled before a vicious kick to his ribs cut off his words and made him double over in a protective curl.

The gratuitous assaults could have proved fatal to the frail old man, but luck bordering on the miraculous, he would later reflect, was with him—he thought of the old saying he remembered hearing from his sainted mother about God looking out for pregnant women and drunks—and Bullet suddenly appeared from nowhere.

Even from his curled, fetal position lying in the doorway, Old Mac could see that the three young punks were big, with one being thin but the other two, brawny. The speed and ferocity with which Bullet attacked them took them all by surprise.

"What the fuck?" one exclaimed before Bullet head-butted him and he went down in a heap, falling across Old Mac's legs. Karate chops and kicks were now flying from Bullet's hands and feet as his body moved in flashing outbursts of deadly agility, hitting the most vulnerable spots on the two remaining opponents who quickly joined their companion, forming a huge, moaning mass in the doorway.

Old Mac was now fully awake and instantly sober, bearing witness to the devastation heaped on his three attackers. What he would never forget-- and no matter how many times he recounted this story to a rapt audience of fellow vagrants, he always stressed-- was the focused intensity on Bullet's face as he methodically but quickly dispatched the three punks. "They never had a chance," Old Mac would chuckle as he reached the climax of his recounting, "and they didn't know what hit 'em." His listeners, quietly impressed, would nod.

Bullet had yanked Old Mac up from the doorway as though he were picking up a piece of paper. Gazing fixedly on the three supine bodies, he spoke in a low, deadly calm voice.

"You like to kick, huh?" Then he delivered a short, brutal kick to the groin of each foe. Cries of anguish echoed down the street as Bullet, practically carrying Old Mac with one arm, took him to a safe area where they both could crash for the night. When Old Mac woke up the next morning, Bullet was gone.

In the weeks and months to come, Old Mac told this story again and again, substituting Scott's real name with the new street name that Old Mac had given him: Bullet. The other street folk listened attentively and developed a great respect for the quiet, elusive Iraq veteran. They also concluded that Old Mac was under Bullet's special protection and gave the old man more respect and a wide berth.

Now, as Old Mac hurried toward Bullet sitting on a bench in the park, his voice was high and excited.

"Someone's lookin' for ya," he said, sitting down next to Bullet and struggling to catch his breath.

Bullet kept his face turned in the direction of the early morning sun and made no response.

"I met Crazy Meg last night at the church soup kitchen, and she told me she heard it from Joe Gimp." Old Mac paused, still struggling to return to a normal breathing rhythm. Bullet didn't move and said nothing. "Who do you think it could be?" Old Mac asked, his voice reflecting both excitement and concern.

"Don't know," Bullet finally said laconically. "Was it a man or a woman?"

"Don't know," Old Mac said, surprised that this fundamental piece of information had not been conveyed in the passed-on message.

Bullet shifted his gaze and seemed to be studying the buildings on the other side of the park. Old Mac observed his young friend's face but couldn't decode his intense expression.

"We could find Joe Gimp and he could tell us somethin' more," Old Mac suggested.

Bullet continued his stare and finally said, "No. We'll run into Joe Gimp soon enough. We don't have to go looking for him."

Old Mac nodded.

Bullet's indifference—at least that's what it seemed to be but, with Bullet, you could never be sure—suggested to Old Mac that whoever was looking for his friend was not anyone Bullet was interested in meeting. Old Mac understood this attitude.

Most street people had become loners when they gave up on and renounced any role in society, cutting loose from all former ties of family and friends. Their reasons were many: alcoholism, business failures, psychological problems, personal tragedy or a total feeling of defeat and worthlessness. They became isolates, drifting from one place to another, or aimlessly navigating the streets of a big city, anonymous except for an assumed street name and a casual interaction with other street regulars.

With Old Mac it was a dead-end job, two failed marriages, a dead child and an unconquerable love for drink. But Old Mac could never pinpoint any specific issues with Bullet that might have made him take to the streets. He hardly ever drank; didn't even smoke. Unlike many street people who would happily tell you their hard-luck stories, Bullet never talked about himself. The only part of his biography that Old Mac knew was that he had served in the Iraq War and had been shot in the head.

Bullet didn't panhandle or collect bottles for their return deposit—two pastimes that Old Mac engaged in to get money for booze. Bullet had a post office box and Old Mac knew that he got a check around the fifteenth of every month because that's when the old man could hit him up for a few bucks. Old Mac speculated that Bullet might be getting a disability pension.

Naturally taciturn, the only question Bullet ever asked of others was if they had served in the military and if so, had they seen any action. Yet he never spoke about the action he had seen. Something in his tense manner and hooded gaze suggested to Old

Mac and others that he must have seen some pretty intense stuff, because he always seemed wound up, like a tightly coiled spring; someone constantly on guard and to be wary of. But Old Mac had seen another side of Bullet on the night Bullet had come to his rescue with the three young punks—not just the lightning speed and fearless ferocity of Bullet's counter-attack, but, later, the tenderness with which he examined the old man for injuries and made sure he was comfortable and secure for the night before leaving him the next morning.

"Come on. I'll buy you breakfast," Bullet said, rising from the park bench and stretching. Old Mac knew that the topic of the person looking for Bullet was now closed. He eagerly accepted Bullet's invitation and the two men walked to a nearly cafeteria and ate breakfast in silence. After that, they parted.

Old Mac's interactions with his young friend were always sporadic and by chance, owing to Bullet's clear desire for a solitary life and Old Mac's frequent binges. Bullet was seen occasionally consorting with the hookers on Clark Street, but even among this group the word was that he was a mostly silent, get-it-over-with guy who never sought the services of the same girl and always had the cash in hand.

When Old Mac sobered up after his latest binge, he went to the First Congregational Church basement to get a free shirt and another pair of pants since his current attire was filthy, and here he ran into Joe Gimp.

"Did that girl ever find Bullet?" Joe Gimp asked casually as he tried on a pair of used tennis shoes.

"What girl?" Old Mac replied.

"The girl who was lookin' for him. She had a picture of Bullet in his army uniform, all spit and polish. I almost didn't recognize him."

"I don't know," Old Mac confessed. "The last time I saw him I gave him the message, but he didn't seem too eager to see anybody."

Joe Gimp tossed the tennis shoes back into a bin and pulled out a pair of worn work boots.

"She said she was his sister," Joe Gimp said.

"His sister?" Old Mac repeated, his interest aroused.

"That's what she said," Joe Gimp replied, lacing up the work boots that looked several sizes too big. "I can stuff these with newspaper and they'll fit fine," Joe Gimp announced, pleased with his find and giving no more attention to the subject of the searching sister as he walked around the basement with his pronounced limp. But Old Mac was interested in why Bullet's sister was searching for him and, even more important, how would Bullet react to this news. Old Mac resolved that he would share this news with his friend when next they met, but there wasn't any rush.

Several days later, mid-morning of a typically drizzly day in Seattle, Old Mac was in a happy mood as he sat on the steps of an old city administration building whose imposing columned porch offered him protection from the rain. He had roused himself early and started scavenging for cans and bottles. The pickings had been good and he had redeemed two trash bags filled to overflowing, dragging them to the redemption center. From there he made a forced march to the nearest liquor store and purchased a pint of his favorite, cheap booze. He was sitting at the end of the columned porch, far away from the entrance to the building, hoping to make himself inconspicuous, sneaking gulps of the warm, soothing liquor concealed in a paper bag. He didn't notice the woman approaching him until she was standing by his side—the side of his bad eye.

"Excuse me," she said in a soft voice conveying both hesitancy and shyness. Instinctively, Old Mac slipped the paper bag containing the liquor under his arm before turning his head and looking up in the direction of the voice.

"Excuse me," she said again.

Old Mac saw a petite young woman, late twenties he guessed, conservatively dressed, a pretty face framed by short brown hair, with eyes that had a distracted, far-off look.

""I'm looking for my brother," the soft voice continued with a tremulous edge, "and I wonder if you might have seen him."

The young woman produced a wallet-size photo from her purse as she spoke and extended it toward Old Mac's field of vision. He looked at the picture of a young man in military dress uniform. It was unmistakably Bullet, without the beard and disheveled clothes that he currently sported. It was the eyes mostly that instantly made him recognizable to Old Mac: the same haunting intensity; same severe expression around the mouth.

"This was taken just before his last tour of duty in Iraq," she said, searching Old Mac's face for any sign of recognition. "He was completing his third tour when he was wounded."

Old Mac stared at the picture, trying to give no hint of recognition as his mind, filled with conflicting thoughts, raced. Did Bullet, who never made reference to any family, want to see his sister? Most street people had, out of shame or bitterness or frustration, intentionally severed all ties to their past lives and usually didn't want to be reminded of them. Did Old Mac have the right to make any decision for the intensely private Bullet and lead his sister to him?

These thoughts whirled about his foggy brain, made fuzzier by the booze he had already consumed that morning. With a blank face he looked up at the young woman and asked, "What makes you think your brother's here in Seattle?"

She broke into a brief, warm smile. "Since he disappeared, every year on our mother's birthday he sends her a card and several of them have had a Seattle postmark." She paused, and her smile faded. "My mother's very sick. She isn't expected to live much longer—really only a matter of a few months. It would mean so much to her to see him again. That's all she talks about, all she's praying for."

Now she gazed off into the rain-soaked horizon and her voice faded into a tone of reverie. "He probably doesn't want to see me, after everything that's happened...but it would mean a lot to her and I just thought maybe there's a chance..." Her voice trailed off and, with an embarrassed half-smile, she returned her gaze to Old Mac. The old man was intrigued by her vague reference to "everything that's happened."

His sentimental side was winning the battle of his conflicting thoughts and, deciding on a hedging tactic, he stood up. Pointing to the picture she still held in her hand he said, "I can't say for sure, mind you, but that picture looks a little bit like a fella I've seen around here." He saw the glimmer of hope flashing in her eyes and didn't want to trap himself, or Bullet. "It's only a small resemblance, really."

"Do you know where I could find him?" she asked quickly, excitement creeping into her voice.

Old Mac resolved to proceed with caution.

"No, I can't rightly say," he responded. "We don't keep to any schedules, you know," he said, and there was an awkward silence as they both confronted the rootlessness of being homeless.

"My name is April," she said, still with residual excitement in her voice, which made Old Mac wonder if somehow, unexpectedly, he had conveyed more than he wished to. She rummaged through her purse and extracted a small notepad and a ballpoint pen. Hastily she scribbled something on the top page.

"I'm staying at the Horizon Hotel over on Jefferson Street. Here's the phone number and my room number. I'll be there for four more days until the end of the week." She tore the page from the notebook and handed it to him with another soft, hopeful half-smile. A clear note of urgency crept into her voice. "If you see the man who resembles the picture, would you ask him if he has a sister named April, and our mother's name is Carol. Ask him to call me, please."

Old Mac glanced at the piece of paper she had handed him. He saw the name Scott at the top of the page and now there was no doubt. Still, his natural wariness told him to remain noncommittal. She was reaching into her purse again. Extracting a leather wallet, she suddenly looked embarrassed. "Can I give you something for your trouble?" she asked tentatively as she withdrew a twenty-dollar bill from the bills neatly tucked in their snug compartment.

His eyes danced excitedly at the prospect of how much booze he could get with this generous offer, but then his better angel reminded him of how his friend Bullet had come to his rescue with the three punks, and all the meals and booze money Bullet had generously offered him through the last several years. He couldn't take money from his friend's sister, could he? The temptation was great.

"No, that's okay," he said half-reluctantly, and watched forlornly as she returned the bill to her wallet.

"Well, thank you," she said, reaching for his hand in a warm, spontaneous gesture. "You won't forget?"

Genuinely touched, Old Mac shook his head. "I won't forget," he repeated.

"Would you mind telling me your name?" she asked timidly.

"Folks call me Old Mac."

"Old Mac," she repeated with inherent dignity

She flashed him a full smile mixing hope and gratitude and then quickly descended the rain-washed steps and, holding the collar of her coat tightly against her slender neck, took quick, long strides to the corner and disappeared from view.

Old Mac folded the piece of paper and placed it deep in his pants pocket—the one without the hole. He lifted the paper bag with the whiskey to his lips and took a long swig. Feeling suddenly like a man elevated by a noble mission, he resolved to find Bullet as quickly as possible and, ignoring the rain, hurried out from the sheltered porch, down the steps and into the freshly chilled air.

* * * *

Old Mac stayed sober—at least half-sober—the next two days while on his mission to find Bullet. He toured all the places where he had previously encountered his friend, to no avail. Then, on the evening of the second day after he met April, he finally saw Bullet in front of an all-night diner where they had occasionally had breakfast together, and he called to him. Bullet stopped and waited for Old Mac to catch up to him.

"What's up?" Bullet asked at Old Mac's approach. "You look all riled up."

Excited about completing his mission, without any preamble Old Mac blurted out, "I met your sister."

Bullet's look instantly changed from casual to intense as his mouth turned down at the corners and his eyes seemed to grow darker. He said nothing.

"She's lookin' for ya because your Mom's dyin' and wants to see you again."

Bullet's jaw muscles were now twitching spasmodically and his eyebrows descended to form a lid over his eyes. His face had turned a blotchy purple, and Old Mac thought for a split second that Bullet was going to hit him. He had seen Bullet's ferocious attacks and didn't want to be his latest victim.

"I didn't tell her I knew ya," he said quickly, holding out his arms like a supplicant and talking rapidly to diffuse any aggression that Bullet might direct at him. "She doesn't know for sure if you're still in Seattle. She's just goin' by the postmark on the birthday card you sent your mother. She showed me a picture of you in uniform and I only said it had a little resemblance to someone I'd seen around but I never identified it as you."

Bullet stood rigidly in one spot, clenching and unclenching his fists. Old Mac dug into his pants pocket and produced the piece of paper that April had written on.

"She asked me to give you this," he said, thrusting the paper at Bullet's chest.

Still silent, Bullet raised one arm and accepted the paper. Jaw muscles still twitching, he read the note. Old Mac didn't know what to expect next.

"You can just throw it away if that's what you want," he suggested, hoping to relieve the tension swirling around them. "She'll just think it was the wrong guy or I never ran into ya. She'll never know. Anyway, she's goin' back home in a few more days."

A look of stark anguish invaded Bullet's face with such suddenness that Old Mac literally took a few steps back, fearful of what his friend's next move might be. Bullet turned, walked over to the end of the sidewalk and sat down on the curb, burying his head in his folded arms. Old Mac now thought Bullet might cry, which would be entirely out of character for this fierce young man, but Bullet just sunk his head lower within his arms and remained totally silent and still.

Feeling that he was out of danger from any antagonism Bullet might have directed toward him as the messenger, Old Mac went over and sat by his friend, joining him in silence. After several minutes Old Mac grew restless and reached in his pocket for his bottle. He took two good swigs before Bullet raised his head and finally spoke.

"My sister doesn't like me because I left my wife and baby daughter," he said, with a hundred-mile stare and a low voice.

Old Mac was fascinated by this revelation but also felt proud that Bullet was making it to him. The old man took another swig of his booze and then, in an unusual gesture befitting these unusual circumstances, moved his bottle directly into Bullet's field of vision.

"You sure ya won't have some?" he offered magnanimously—he never shared his drink with anyone. Bullet pushed the bottle away and continued staring across the street at some imaginary ghost.

"You must have had your reasons," Old Mac said gravely, hoping to coax Bullet to tell him more. In a steely, disembodied voice Bullet now spoke as if he were reliving the scenes and events he began to describe.

"I kept going back to Iraq and putting my ass on the line because I couldn't settle down to life at home. I was nervous and jumpy and angry all the time. I was like a junkie—I needed the adrenalin rush of fighting and living every day on the edge, facing the real possibility of getting killed: a sniper's bullet, an I.E.D., an ambush. But then, comes the end of the day and you're still standin', you feel so alive, so competent and fuckin' powerful. And all my platoon buddies knew they could count on me to cover their back and I could depend on them. I loved those guys. We were all tight and when one of us took a bullet or went down, it was like losing a member of your family. It made you want to fight even more."

Bullet paused and gave a sidelong glance at Old Mac who was shaking his head in affirmation of everything Bullet said. In his hazy state the old man imagined that he, too, had experienced similar reactions to fighting in Korea, forgetting that he was a supply corporal who never saw the enemy in any kind of combat. Bullet continued.

"After I was wounded on my third tour, I couldn't go back any more but I couldn't settle down, couldn't settle for a peaceful, quiet life with my wife and little girl in our cramped, rented house, with my boring job in the window factory. I went crazy. I couldn't control my anger or my frustration."

Bullet stopped and looked down at the curb before continuing in a lower voice. "I even hit Angie, my wife, which is something I never thought I'd ever do." Bullet stopped again and started running his fingers through his hair in quick, jerky strokes.

"You guys had it rough over there," Old Mac said with boozy conviction. Bullet uttered a weak grunt before continuing.

"Angie was afraid I'd hurt the baby so she went to stay with my sister, April. I wasn't sleepin'. After all that action in Iraq I was an adrenalin junkie and couldn't calm down and function at a normal, civilian pace. I was takin' a lot of pills and seein' an army shrink, but nothing was helping me. Every day was a battle just to get out of the fuckin' bed and go through the boring daily routines. Nobody understood. My sister was pissed at me. My mother was ringin' her hands and cryin' a lot."

"What about your father?" Old Mac asked.

"He died when I was twelve. It was just my Mom, my sister and me, until I married Angie. She was April's best friend."

"Sorry about your father," Old Mac said.

"Anyway," Bullet said in the same deep, far-off voice, "one day after work when I'd just gotten chewed out by the fuckin' foreman for fighting with another guy, I went to April's house to see my daughter. As soon as I walked into her room, she started screamin'. She was obviously frightened of me. I can't say I blamed her. She was only two and she had seen some pretty scary shit between Angie and me. But that was it for me. I couldn't take any more. I left town that night and never went back."

Bullet's voice trailed off. He hugged his knees and continued staring far into space.

"But your sister ain't mad at you now," Old Mac said, trying to be reassuring. "Otherwise, she wouldn't be tryin' to find ya."

Bullet seemed to be considering Old Mac's observation before answering. "She's always been very close to my mother. She's doing this for her."

Old Mac was now thinking of his own mother through a boozy, sentimental haze. While his mother had been worn out by the time he arrived, the fifth of seven children, ground down by poverty and his own father's drinking and checkered work record, Old Mac now fondly recalled the few times his mother had given him any special attention.

"No one loves ya like your mother," he announced with watery eyes and a weak smile. Encouraged by Bullet's silence, he dared to go a bit further. "I wish I could see my ma one more time," he said, filled with self-pity, "but she died a long time ago."

Bullet now looked down at the piece of paper that Old Mac had given him and read the brief note from April again.

"Why don't ya go see your sister?" Old Mac said, hoping to encourage a family reconciliation, forgetting how he had long ago severed ties with all of his six siblings. Caught up in the emotions of the moment, he longed for his young friend to recapture that which would never be possible for him. Then he saw the deep pain etched on Bullet's face.

Without speaking, Bullet rose from the curb and started walking away. Even in his tipsy condition Old Mac instantly sensed that the wall was up around Bullet and it was impenetrable. He didn't follow his friend but sat on the curb drinking some more and pondering the sad state of man's wretchedness. His maudlin thoughts continued apace with his drinking. Before long he was openly crying and blubbering mawkish sentiments about family, to the amusement of the passersby.

* * * *

For several days Bullet had not been seen, either by Old Mac or any of the street regulars when Old Mac inquired of his friend. Then on a sunny, early May morning, as Old Mac was leaving the Methodist church hall after enjoying a hot meal, he ran into Crazy Meg. Her gray hair in total disarray, a man's felt hat perched precariously on the side of her head, and a ratty sweater worn backwards over a long, woolen nightgown, Crazy Meg seemed to fit her street name perfectly. But Old Mac knew that the old lady cultivated this crazy, disheveled appearance as a protective device, since a lot of people were spooked by folks who looked or acted strangely and stayed away from them. As soon as she saw him, Crazy Meg hustled over to Old Mac's side and spoke in an excited voice.

"I saw that lady who was lookin' for Bullet," she announced. "But this time she was lookin' for you."

Old Mac shot her a quizzical look.

"She was leavin' Seattle and wanted to thank you for findin' her brother."

Old Mac broke out in a boozy smile. ""So she found her brother," he said, pleased that he had played a part in this reunion.

"No, that's the strange part," Meg said quickly. "She never saw her brother. She asked me to tell you, if I seen you, that her mother got her wish and to thank you."

"But she never got to see him?" Bullet asked, amazed.

"From what she said, No," Crazy Meg said placidly "But it didn't seem to bother her. She was just glad that her mother got her wish, whatever that was. She didn't say." Crazy Meg cocked her head. "Maybe Bullet owed her money."

Old Mac gave her a knowing look, shook his head and wandered off. In a distracted state he walked for several blocks until he came to a small park and sat on a rusted bench, ignoring the noisy pigeons that flocked about him.

A long scowl on his stubbly face betrayed the concentration deep inside his foggy, half-pickled brain. Accustomed to thinking only about the best ways of getting food, shelter and liquor for the day, his brain was now on overdrive. Eventually he was rewarded with what passed for a logical explanation of recent events, and a small, crinkly smile crept across his weathered face.

Bullet had left Seattle and gone back to see his mother one more time. He had not made contact with his sister because she was aligned with his wife and he didn't want to open that can of worms. Mental pictures of Bullet at his dying mother's bedside made Old Mac tear up. But that's where the pictures ended. It was probably the mother's dying wish that Bullet come back home and be reconciled with his wife and daughter and sister, but instinct told Old Mac that such a happy ending was impossible for Bullet.

Even with his limited experience in Korea, Old Mac knew something about war and soldiers and fighting and the constant presence of death and what it did to some guys in permanently screwing up their heads. This dark knowledge made him understand intuitively why Bullet could never settle into the mainstream of civilian life; could never adapt to the ordinary expectations of job and home and family; could never endure a life that other men took for granted and found pleasure and peace in. No, Bullet would be back in Seattle any day now. The ties loosely forged by the undemanding confederation of street people were his links to a life that allowed him the freedom to fight his demons privately, with no recriminations, no moralizing and no pity.

Certain that he would see his friend again, Old Mac smiled, stretched and turned his attention to the elemental needs of the day.

Too Good To Be True

Dear Curtis,

You'll probably think it strange to be hearing from me since I'm sure I'm the last person you want to be writing you, given all the publicity that's surrounded my name lately. So I apologize in advance but you are my only relative even if we're only half brothers and we grew up in different states and were never close as adults. Still I've got to tell someone my side of the story which couldn't come out in the trial because my lawyer said it made no sense and would only prejudice the jury against me. He considered an insanity plea but decided against it, saying that juries seldom went for that.

I guess I should start at the beginning. Soon after I finished my second tour of duty in Afghanistan and was discharged from the army I met Johanna at a counseling session for returning vets who were having trouble adjusting back into civilian life. My head was really screwed up. I couldn't sleep and kept having flashbacks to ugly scenes in the war. I suffered frequent, intense headaches. I was having anger management issues, had lost two jobs and was drinking pretty heavily. Johanna was the counselor running my group.

I have to admit I felt an instant attraction—soft brown eyes, a sweet smile, nice body and long, shapely legs—and the good looks you and I both inherited from our Dad had an instant effect on her, she told me later. Anyway, I wasn't looking for any romance or serious relationship. I just wanted to stop feeling so angry all the time.

Johanna seemed to take a special interest in me. After a group session was over and the other guys were drifting out, she'd come over to me with a big, bright smile and ask me how I was doing. We'd have a private chat for a few minutes and she'd listen with a lot of attention, shaking her head and smiling as I began to open up to her.

One night after a session in which I was sharing how angry I was at a neighbor in my apartment building for playing his music so loud late at night and refusing to turn it down that I wanted to rip his throat out, Johanna suggested we go someplace for coffee. That's when I discovered how special she was. She was warm and witty and upbeat and understanding and sympathetic. I found myself really letting go and telling her all the things that were bothering me. Every now and then she'd sneak in some comment or suggestion that helped me to get a handle on my feelings.

We talked for over two hours--actually I did most of the talking—until the coffee shop closed. For the first time since my discharge I felt calm, peaceful. It was like I had found someone to share my troubles with, someone who really cared and had a positive effect on me.

After our next group session I asked her out for coffee and she readily agreed. That's how it started, Curtis. We'd go for coffee and sit and talk for hours. The more I learned about her, the more I liked her. She was two years older then me and was a licensed counselor with a full-time job working for the city. She came from a big family someplace out in Montana, real pioneer stock. She told me she had been briefly married before but her husband committed suicide. I wanted to ask her more about that but she clearly didn't want to talk about it and I could understand that so I dropped it.

Johanna belonged to some evangelical group and seemed to be deeply religious. Now I've never been a church goer, just like our Dad, but from the way she talked, her faith was at the center of her life and I liked that about her. I guess I could sum it up by saying she was peaceful and calm—all the things I wasn't at this point in my life—and I was drawn to her. She had a soothing effect on me. All my anger and frustration seemed to just float away when I was with her.

I finally got up the courage to ask her out on a real date and she said yes. We had a good time on that first date although I noticed she didn't like my cussing. She didn't come right out and say it but she'd wince a little if I said goddamn. So I tried to keep the swearing to a minimum which after three and a half years of living with guys in Afghanistan wasn't easy.

We started going out regularly and every time I was with her, I felt good. She said she was praying for me and I believed her. She invited me to her church but I was honest with her and said that I just wasn't into religion of any kind. She didn't press me. She'd just smile and say, "I'll keep praying."

She was a damn attractive woman and I had a real itch for her but she let me know in no uncertain terms that she wasn't jumping in the sack with me unless we made a firm commitment to each other and I figured she meant marriage.

After about six months I was beginning to feel pretty good about myself. I had a new job as a carpenter on a construction crew for a big builder. I liked the guys on my crew and was making progress in managing my anger although I still attended the vets' sessions, mostly to be near her. My drinking was under control and even my headaches were better—not so intense and not so frequent. I started night classes at the local community college to get the degree I had been pursuing before I dropped out and joined the army.

I decided that Johanna was the best thing that ever happened to me and I was ready to make the kind of commitment she wanted. I popped the question and she said yes and we got married.

I moved into her apartment and at first everything was great. I'm not saying we didn't have any of the typical problems that young married couples have. Johanna was very neat and I'm a slob and I could see how much my sloppiness bothered her. She was forever picking up after me but she never said anything. Like after I took a shower and left the bathroom, she'd rush in and pick up the towel I left on the floor and throw my dirty shorts in the hamper and straighten everything up. I drank a lot of coffee—an old army habit—and if I left a coffee cup sitting someplace around the apartment on a weekend, when I'd look for it, she would have already emptied it and washed it.

Her apartment was filled with religious pamphlets and books on Jesus and now that I was living with her I could see how seriously she took her religion. She'd get up very early each morning and spend about an hour studying The Bible or reading about Jesus. I thought this was a little excessive but, what the hell, if this is what made her the good person she was, read on! As I said, things were going great for the first six months but then everything started to go downhill.

A new supervisor was assigned to my work crew and right away he and I didn't get along. He knew I was an Afghanistan vet and he started making cracks that only idiots volunteered for the army and were willing to die so big corporations could make huge profits in keeping oil pumping to America. I tried to ignore him but he kept needling me until I couldn't stand it any more. I went crazy and punched him out and broke his nose. I was fired and told I'd never get a reference for another job.

When I told Johanna that I had lost my job, she looked deflated for a minute but then she smiled. "You'll find another one--a better one," she said, patting me on the shoulder.

The weeks went by and I didn't find another job and I stopped going to school and started to drink again. Johanna would come home from work and find me some days in my bathrobe, just watching television and drinking beer. Right away she'd collect all the beer cans and start cleaning up the living room. I'd be in a sour mood and feeling angry with myself so I'd take it out on her and start yelling and telling her our place felt more like a model apartment than a real home and why didn't she leave things alone? She'd just smile and continue cleaning up

"What would you like for dinner?" she'd ask brightly, but most of the time when I had been drinking all day, I didn't want anything to eat.

She never argued with me or hollered at me. She'd just give me a look that told me how disappointed in me she was. That look would make me furious because I didn't need her to tell me what a shit I was. I was filled with self-disgust and seeing the disappointment in her eyes just made me feel worse, so I drank more and got angrier and started hollering at her for the slightest thing.

I started smoking again—I had given it up when I came back from Afghanistan—and I knew she hated the smell of cigarette smoke as well as the mess I made with overflowing ashtrays. Still, she never said a word about the mess. She'd just say, "Smoking is really bad for you," and I'd explode with a lot of verbal abuse and she'd retreat to the bedroom in silence.

She asked me to go to church with her but I refused. She started spending more time reading her Bible and her religious books. I was in a downward spiral as my anger and frustration overwhelmed me. My headaches got worse and my drinking increased. She begged me to attend the vet's meetings and suggested I should join another group where she wasn't the facilitator. In desperation I did join another group and after a bad drinking binge I started going to AA meetings. I knew I had a long, long road to recovery but I had hit rock bottom and had nowhere to go but up.

I finally sobered up and I got a job with a small general contractor and things were looking up again. Johanna could not have been more supportive. She was constantly telling me, "I'm so proud of how you're tackling your problems."

Curtis, here's where the tricky part comes in. I don't to this day fully understand it myself. All I can say is that our relationship changed and I started seeing Johanna in a strange new light. I was her cross that she bore patiently, uncomplainingly, like Christ bore his cross. My sins and imperfections were challenging her to become a better person.

If I swore, if I lost my temper, if I fell off the wagon, if I was verbally sarcastic, if I got in a fight with anyone, if I lost a job, if I made a mess in the apartment or took up smoking again, she responded to all my actions passively, calmly. I started to believe in my gut that she welcomed my repeated failures as a means of testing her to become a better person. I no longer saw any hurt in her eyes. I imagined that I saw almost a gleam, welcoming yet another challenge from me that she would heroically bear. Then I started to believe that she fully expected me to fail and even **wanted** me to fail because that suited her higher purpose. She had taken me on as her personal cross.

I became paranoid, feeling that she was watching me all the time with those calm, calculating eyes, waiting for me to disappoint her, to fail, to offer her another trial. For all her soothing words and kind encouragements, she was being the long suffering, saintly wife to this poor, wretched sinner who could **never** live up to her standards but **could** be the path to her salvation.

Curtis, I don't know if you ever saw the movie called The Picture of Dorian Gray, but it's about a handsome young man who makes a pact with the devil and sells his soul to remain forever young and unchanged in appearance. No matter what evil crimes he commits through the years, the effects of his sins are revealed only in a portrait of him, hidden away where he alone can view it and see how his sinful life would age him. His physical appearance never ages, never changes. As the years pass and he occasionally looks at the hidden portrait, he is horrified to see the grotesquely ugly person he has really become.

I mention this movie because in some strange, unexplainable way, whenever I looked into Johanna's eyes I saw only my mounting imperfections, my sins and failures. To all outward appearances she was the perfect wife—dedicated, supportive and loving. To me she was now my personal demon, expecting me to fail and secretly welcoming my failures. My anger and resentment mushroomed.

You can ask why I just didn't pick up and leave her but the strange twist is that I knew I couldn't make it on my own and there was some desperate part of me that still loved her. I was trapped. I was living with a woman who was a saint but whose very presence only highlighted all my shortcomings. I saw her eyes everywhere, watching me, assessing me, challenging me, tolerating me.

"I'm praying for you," she would tell me all the time, her eyes sparkling with smug virtue.

I lost another job and started drinking again. Still no complaints from Mother Teresa, only quiet toleration. I came home drunk that fateful night and my head was exploding with pain. I found her sitting in bed reading her Bible. She stopped her reading as I staggered toward the bed and calmly said "Hello darling," with a slight smile and those eyes boring through me, assessing my condition, despising me for my weaknesses but welcoming another chance to prove how forgiving and faithful she was. Her eyes condemned me to see what a wretched person I was and always would be. They seemed to float out of her head, multiplying in number and increasing in size until they were surrounding me, mocking me. The pain in my head was so sharp that I was squinting at all those eyes around me. I remembered being in Afghanistan on duty at night, imagining the eyes of the enemy all around me. I had to blot those eyes out.

I remember rushing toward the bed and screaming "Stop it! Stop it!" I grabbed a pillow and put it over her head to shield me from those eyes that were judging me, condemning me. I was screaming incoherently now because I still saw all those eyes and I buried my head in the side of the pillow to blot out those fearful, accusing images. I heard some muffled sounds and felt Johanna's hands pushing against my arms, but then I must have blacked out. When I came to, everything was silent and still. Only a slim pillow separated me from Johanna's lifeless face.

At the trial my lawyer stressed my war record and my post-traumatic stress but the prosecutor depicted me as an alcoholic who couldn't hold a job and was subject to violent fits of rage. Johanna was pictured as a loving, kind, faithful wife and of course she was all those things and I never meant to kill her.

Here's the funny part, Curtis. As I sit in my cell day after day I keep asking myself why Johanna's first husband committed suicide. What role did this perfect wife have in his decision? And here's another thought I have that sounds crazy, I know, but keeps looping through my head. Johanna reached her ultimate goal of perfection. She gave her life rather than compromise her standards. She was a martyr. I bet she's up in heaven now, smiling down on me with loving forgiveness. I still see her eyes watching me all the time. Last week I had another episode and wound up in a padded cell again. I can't escape her. She's in heaven and I'm in hell.

Thanks for listening. If you're ever in this area, drop by. I'm always home. Ha Ha!

Jerry

Albert Resurgent

The day Brother Albert passed away was a sad day for everyone in our monastery but especially for me.

The abbot made the announcement at the start of our evening meal, casting a pall over everyone's mood. While we believe in an eternal life and our liturgy celebrates the passing of a holy soul to God's embrace, we are still human and miss the company of cherished companions. The abbot had led us in a brief prayer for the soul of the departed and I thought I heard his voice falter once or twice.

Brother Albert had been suffering terribly from a slow-moving, all-consuming cancer devouring one organ after another. Still, he had persevered in performing his duties until the pain and weariness and emaciation overwhelmed him and he was removed to the hospital. We all knew that his death was imminent but, even so, the stark announcement of his passing gave me a jolt, and a flood of memories came pouring into my mind.

At that time I was a relative newcomer to the monastic life, having been at Holy Cross Monastery for not quite three years when Brother Albert died. At twenty-seven I was still having a fierce internal debate about taking holy orders and questioning if I was really suited for this life. Part of me felt drawn to the tranquil regimen of work, prayer and contemplation, but another part of me wanted adventure and discovery and a broader canvas on which to make my imprint. A more fundamental problem, that I only shared with my spiritual advisor, the abbot, was fluctuating doubts about God's personal relationship with man. All in all, I was mightily confused and constantly questioning my future in the religious life.

"It's not uncommon for a young man to have these conflicted feelings, Robert," the abbot had told me at our last spiritual conference when I confessed my uncertainty.

"Sometimes, Reverend Father, I think I'm just too worldly and will never be able to cut off, or at least subdue, my interest in things of the world."

"Few men come to our way of life without having to grapple with renouncing other dreams and desires. For some it's easier than for others. It takes time. Pray hard, Robert, and the answers will eventually come to you."

I had been assigned to work in the kitchen garden with Brother Albert and immediately saw him as a quiet, gentle soul, at peace with himself and his chosen place in the world. Yet he also possessed warmth and a sparkle that was glimpsed by the twinkle in his eyes and a steady stream of smiles that animated his angular face. I admired this older man tremendously and hoped to pattern my religious life on his.

Our monastic rule discouraged forming special friendships, but that didn't mean you couldn't enjoy the company of certain brothers during our evening social hour in the common room. While I never shunned any brother, for that would be a serious breach of our rule, I always made an effort to be in Brother Albert's orbit. He laughed easily and often, yet it seemed to me that there was a natural reticence, a calm inner core to him that I, who was always in turmoil, envied.

While other men talked about their childhoods and families and life experiences up to their arrival at the monastery, Brother Albert was silent on his background and was content to be an appreciative listener and to keep the conversation going with pertinent questions. Though not quite sixty, he was clearly much admired and liked by everyone in our community, but he wore this leadership mantle lightly, even humbly.

His strength and forbearance and endless good humor in facing his pain and deterioration seemed to enlarge his soul while ravaging his body, until he was reduced to pure spirit. He never lost his calm inner core, which I construed to be his unshakable faith—a steadiness of purpose and clarity of belief which, at that time, I felt I would never possess. His manner of dying was therefore for me further evidence of my own shallow convictions, casting more doubt on my suitability for monastic life.

At my next spiritual conference with my abbot, I talked about Brother Albert as the model of a holy life and again expressed my doubts about myself. Reverend Father listened attentively as I droned on about all my unresolved conflicts between participating in the world and retreating from it.

"You shouldn't view our way of life as an escape from the world, Robert," the abbot said with benign patience. "It's not a 'running from' but a 'running to,' because we ultimately decide that this path brings us greater spiritual fulfillment."

"Maybe I'm just too disposed to the things of the world," I confessed with a spasm of self-pity. "I saw Brother Albert as someone who only had allegiance to God and this monastery, pure and simple. I wish I could be like him. I pray and pray, but I don't think I will ever attain his inner peace, his total acceptance."

Reverend Father shot me a consoling smile as he shifted in his chair.

"And you think that this inner peace, this resignation to God's will, is something that some men have always possessed? Men like Brother Albert?"

"It's possible," I said, not sure of what I thought

"What do you know about Brother Albert's background, Robert?"

"Very little," I admitted. "I know that he didn't come to the monastic life until he was in his thirties and that he was born in Austria. That's about all."

Reverend Father crossed his legs and rearranged his cassock. A tall, handsome man in his mid- sixties, he now looked pensive. His hands rested on his lap and he stared off into the far corner of the room.

"Yes, Brother Albert was born in Austria. He was a Jew. He came from a wealthy Jewish banking family. When he was eleven years old he was sent to Auschwitz with his mother and father and two sisters. When the Allies liberated the camp, he was the only one in his family who had survived."

This startling revelation left me momentarily disoriented, and I had to force myself to attend to the abbot's unfolding history of Brother Albert.

"He had an uncle, Benjamin, who had immigrated to America at the start of Hitler's rise to power, and who arranged to have Albert come to live with him in Pennsylvania. His uncle, also in banking, had prospered and was married to an American girl, an Irish Catholic. They had only one child of their own, a son named David, five years older than Albert, who immediately welcomed his cousin as a younger brother and they grew very close. Benjamin was a non-practicing Jew but his wife, Helen, was a devout Catholic. Albert went to Mass with her and David and read a lot about the Catholic Church. He soon asked to become a convert. Benjamin had no objections since his own son was being raised a Catholic, and Helen was delighted."

Reverend Father paused and took a sip of water from a glass on the table next to his chair. Then he continued.

"Albert loved his uncle and aunt and cousin, loved his new religion and loved his adopted country. The indelibly horrific memories of Auschwitz must have lurked in the dark corners of his eyes, but he possessed a ready smile and a sensitivity to others that won him friends and followers. When America entered the Korean conflict, Albert saw this as a push by the Communists to dominate the world, much in the manner of the Third Reich, so he left college and volunteered for the army. He was sent to Korea as a medic"

I had trouble picturing Brother Albert, so calm and serenely peaceful, in combat, and Reverend Father must have noted the confusion on my face.

"Would it surprise you to know that Albert showed a fierce dedication to his fellow soldiers above and beyond the call of duty and distinguished himself by his bravery? Once, while ministering to a wounded soldier during a raging battle, Albert was shot in the back but managed to crawl over two hundred feet to safety, dragging the wounded soldier with him. Another time he crawled directly across the line of enemy fire to aid a fallen soldier. In all, he was wounded three times but returned to duty after each wound was healed and ended up with a chest full of medals and special commendations: a true hero.

"His physical wounds had all healed but his psychological wounds were festering. He had seen enough death and brutality and inhumanity to challenge any sane person and he needed time to try to make sense of it all."

I shook my head in amazement at all these revelations and Reverend Father smiled again.

"Albert didn't return to college and finish his pre-med program. Instead he went off to a commune in Oregon where he grew his own food and practiced meditation and seemed to go deep within himself to find some satisfactory answers to all that he had seen and experienced. His Uncle Benjamin and Aunt Helen, along with his cousin, David, visited him occasionally during the five years that he was there. They found a man struggling to come to terms with life, grappling with issues of good and evil and searching for inner peace that seemed to elude him. He confided to his cousin that he had lost his faith.

It was hard for me to picture Brother Albert in a continuous state of turmoil, similar to my own, but Reverend Father was authoritatively stating this condition as fact and I never doubted his word, although I did wonder how he knew these intimate details. I answered my own speculation by reasoning that Reverend Father had been Brother Albert's spiritual advisor, too, and much is shared in that relationship.

Reverend Father rose and stood next to his chair.

"Finally, after five years, Albert left the Oregon commune and plunged back into life, working as a paramedic in Los Angeles. His Uncle Benjamin passed away and he returned home to Pennsylvania for the funeral. At that time he shared with David that he was still floundering spiritually, but seemed to be moving toward some peaceful resolution through his work. Ultimately, he found his way back to God and to faith through giving himself to others. Finally, at thirty-three, he had resolved his major issues and that's when he came to our monastery. Still, he found himself wrestling with one unresolved conflict: his wish to retreat from the world and his desire to be of active service to others. Eventually settling his inner struggle, he remained with us."

Reverend Father moved to an overcrowded bookcase at the other end of the room.

"Have you ever read Dante's *Divine Comedy*, Robert?" he asked me, reaching for a book on the top shelf.

"Only a third of it," I replied honestly. "*The Inferno.*"

"Ah, then you must read the other two sections," he said cheerfully, bringing the book to me. "You see, Robert, God's chosen path is not the same for all of us, and we come to Him from different experiences. For some, like Brother Albert, you have to experience Hell as he did in Auschwitz and Korea and walk in darkness and desolation before you can rebuild your faith and make your way back to Him. That's why Dante leads us through Hell and Purgatory before taking us to Heaven. We are all imperfect, but understanding evil and fighting temptation can be His way of leading us to a clearer vision of our purpose in life and our best means of serving Him. Even Dante was in turmoil and despondency when he started his journey."

"Thank you, Reverend Father," I said, taking the book from him and then kneeling for his blessing, grateful for this extraordinary session with him and the hope he gave me through his sharing Brother Albert's surprising history.

Our entire community was performing all the rituals for the dead with a mixture of joy and sadness, and I heard that Brother Albert's aunt had arrived at the monastery to join in some of our ceremonies. I was leaving the refectory when I encountered Reverend Father with a lady who, by her stooped posture and lined face, seemed very old. Reverend Father smiled and beckoned me to his side. Possessed of a natural exuberance, today he was particularly animated.

"Robert, I'd like you to meet my mother, Helen."

* * * *

No matter how many years have elapsed, I still think of Brother Albert and the life-path that brought him to God and a peaceful resolution to his spiritual struggles. He had seen all the horrors that man could inflict on his fellow man through wars and unbridled fanaticism. He had experienced the despair that suffuses the soul with the abandoning of hope and belief. Then, like Dante rising through Hell and Purgatory to the light of Paradise, Albert rose from the depths of desolation to find a renewed purpose in life, a humbler acceptance of man's frailties, and a deeper connection with God.

Brother Albert's story and his indomitable spirit were instrumental in helping me to resolve my own conflicts and select my path. Now that I am abbot, I often pass along Albert's story to young novices who, like me so many years ago, feel themselves at a crossroad as they struggle to choose a direction and take that decisive step toward their spiritual destination.

I feel most humble when my brethren now refer to me as Reverend Father, for I have learned over the course of a long life that it is the humblest among us, like Brother Albert, who are, deservingly, the most revered and, undoubtedly, the closest to God.

Brother Albert's presence abides with us.

Parting Shots

His name was Bobby Lee. He was eleven years old and walked slowly on three legs, the result of a roadside bomb on the outskirts of Baghdad. He was a large-boned German shepherd with soulful black eyes and a tan and black coat that Frank brushed every day because for some reason it seemed to sooth the old dog and reaffirm their bond.

That bond had been forged seven years ago when the dog and Frank had gone through bomb sniffing training together and then spent over a year working as a team in Iraq until the day the multiple explosions ripped their convoy apart, leaving Bobby Lee and Frank badly injured, lying side by side amid the rubble of the flaming Humvee they had been traveling in.

Despite his injuries, the dog's instincts and his love for his master compelled him to save Frank from the exploding flames engulfing them. Unconscious at first, Frank woke up and saw the red and black of shooting flames and thick smoke crowding out the blazing sun. Then he felt Bobby Lee, his jaws gripping Frank's boot, struggling to pull him away from the burning wreckage.

When Frank raised his head to get a clearer picture, he saw one of Bobby Lee's back legs dangling inertly from his body and his thick black coat smoldering along his spine. With fierce concentration the dog was using just three legs to drag his master to safety. Frank never forgot that image.

He felt pain in different parts of his body, so intense that his brain had not yet scanned and reported on the specific wounded spots. Still, he managed to turn over on his belly with one arm—the other one seemed useless, disconnected from the rest of him—and start crawling toward a ditch by the side of the road, with Bobby Lee relaxing his grip on Frank's boot and limping slowly by his side. The smell of burning oil assaulted Frank's nostrils and the moans and cries of other soldiers in the convoy filled his ears. He managed to tumble down into the ditch before blacking out again.

When he came to once more, he was back in the Green Zone's hospital and his first words were, "How's my dog?" The nurse tending him didn't have the slightest idea what he was talking about, thinking maybe while under anesthesia he had been dreaming of some pet he had back home.

Frank repeated his question with an urgent rise to his voice. Seeing the nurse's blank stare, he added, "The dog that was with me when our convoy was hit. He's my partner."

The nurse's expression changed and she smiled. "I don't know but I'll find out."

"Please. Please," he said with even more urgency before he felt himself drifting away.

Some time later, he was conscious of a man in a white coat standing next to his bed, checking his pulse. Seeing Frank's eyes flickering, he spoke. "You're gonna be okay, sergeant, but you may have to give up golf for a while and eat out of one side of your mouth."

"My dog?" Frank muttered.

"Oh, yes, your dog," the doctor said, releasing Frank's wrist. "We just got word. He's okay, too. They had to amputate one of his hind legs and he suffered a lot of burns and some shrapnel wounds, just like you, but he'll survive."

Frank struggled to take in this list of injuries that he and Bobby Lee had sustained. The doctor said, "The good news is, you're both going home."

And home they went, but not together. Frank went to Walter Reed Army Medical Center for operations on his left shoulder and leg, kneecap and hip replacement, skin grafts on face, neck and chest and months of physical therapy. When he wasn't in a drug-induced twilight zone to relieve his pain, he was aware of his mother and his longtime girlfriend, Sally, hovering at his bedside, his mother crying, Sally offering encouraging smiles.

When he finally was allowed out of bed and saw himself in a mirror, he understood why his mother was weeping. His transformation was remarkably grotesque: the facial and body scars; the bald spot just above his left ear—a half-dollar-size patch staring out amidst his thick, close-cropped black hair; the checkerboard skin discoloration where new skin was mixing with old; the off-kilter way his left arm hung away from his body.

He turned his face away in furious disgust and thereafter refused to shave himself in a mirror.

Once all the operations were finished and the long, arduous physical therapy began—two hours, twice a day, six days a week, for months--his black, despairing moods started to lift and most of his thoughts centered on Bobby Lee.

The dog, according to Sally's conscientious reports, was in a veterinary hospital in Virginia, undergoing his own recovery regimen. Then one day, about five months after Frank had been airlifted back to the States, his mother approached his bed. She always appeared to have tearful eyes and today was no exception, but now she also sported a big smile.

"We have a big surprise for you," she said, bending over to kiss him on his blotchy cheek. "Come to the window."

He left his bed and awkwardly made his way to the window where his mother was standing, tears now washing her face.

"Look!" she said, excitement filling her voice, as she pointed down to the grassy area three stories below the window. He squinted against the mid-day sunlight to get a clearer view and caught sight of Sally waving up to him. Then he saw Bobby Lee standing by her side, his ears erect, staring off into the distance as if the dog was trying to decide what he should be focusing on.

Frank followed the curve of his back, resting his eyes on the hip and the missing leg.

Sally was talking to the dog and pointing to Frank's window. Frank quickly raised the window with his good arm, leaned out and called, "Bobby Lee!" The dog's ears turned toward the sound and then his head swiveled and followed the direction of Frank's call. "Bobby Lee!" Frank called again, and the dog looked directly at him. A brief second for recognition and then the dog's body seemed to leave the ground and hang in the air. Now Bobby Lee was barking furiously and turning in awkward, three-legged circles. Then he was straining at the leash, pulling the laughing Sally closer to the building and now interrupting his barks with puppy-like whimpers.

Frank was waving his arm and shouting "Hello, buddy," over and over. His chest tightened and currents welled up in his throat as pure joy electrified his body.

Bobby Lee tried to stand up on his remaining hind leg as if to get closer to Frank and fell over on his side. Undaunted, he repeated this motion, exhausting himself until Frank had to shout, "Bobby Lee, sit!"

The dog's training kicked in and he immediately sat on his haunches, still looking up at Frank, eyes alert, his long pink tongue draped over his muzzle, waiting for another command.

Sally called up, "That's enough for today. Go back to bed." She tried to get Bobby Lee's attention but his eyes would not leave his master. Reluctantly, Frank realized that he would have to leave the window in order for Sally to get the dog back to her car. He walked slowly back toward the bed, gently assisted by his mother, listening to Bobby Lee's frantic whimpering and barks of protest receding in the distance.

Sally and his mother had rented a small house not far from Walter Reed where Bobby Lee was now living. For several days after the reunion, Sally reported that Bobby Lee was refusing to eat and just lying by the front door. After four days the dog finally ate but, Sally reported, he seemed listless and lost. Whenever she picked up the car keys, Bobby Lee's ears would start twitching and he'd rise from his place by the front door and look eagerly at Sally. But Sally and his mother were afraid that further visits to the hospital would only make the dog more depressed by not being able to be with his master.

Fortunately, it was only another month before Frank was officially discharged from the hospital. On that day, doctors, nurses and most of the ambulatory patients on Frank's ward gathered at the windows to witness the reunion of the soldier and his canine partner. Thanks to Frank's mother, who had spread the story of how Bobby Lee selflessly tried to rescue his master from the burning convoy, the dog was considered a hero.

Frank's fellow patients yelled and whooped, the doctors smiled and the nurses cried when Bobby Lee, standing with Sally about fifty feet along the path to the hospital entrance, spotted Frank emerging through the doorway.

Breaking from Sally's hold on his leash, the dog made his crazy hop-jump, half-sideways run toward Frank and, with the miraculous strength of his one remaining hind leg, leaped into Frank's outstretched arms. Knocked off balance, Frank fell on his backside, laughing, crying, gasping, as Bobby Lee licked him furiously.

* * * *

They went back to Georgia, to the town where Frank had grown up, to the house that his grandfather had bought on a G.I. loan after serving in the Navy during WW II, and where his father, now deceased, and mother had spent their married life together. Frank and Sally were married and he loved her for insisting that they stay in the family house where they could offer company to Frank's widowed mother.

His wounds healed, skin grafts gradually blended with surrounding tissue, and Frank's body adjusted to the artificial new parts that had been implanted. His old job at the furniture factory was waiting for him, and he was promoted to supervisor after completing a management program at the local community college. He became a father; first a baby girl, followed two years later with twin boys.

To all appearances he was a happy, contented man. Only Sally knew the dark corners of his mind: the nightmares and early morning shakes; the looming quietness that would come over him at times when his eyes took on a hollow look and seemed to be gazing inward at some far-off scene; the long walks he would insist on taking alone in the deep, piney woods surrounding their house, accompanied always by Bobby Lee.

When Frank was in one of his dark moods, Sally felt shut out. Everyone was shut out except the dog, who seemed to sense his master's feeling and would hover at his side. Sally could never predict when these moods might descend on Frank or what triggered them. They were like summer squalls that abruptly swept across the horizon with no warning.

Sally would come into the living room at night after dinner and find the kids and Frank and his mother watching television. One glance at Frank and she'd know he wasn't watching the TV screen although his eyes gazed opaquely in that direction. Sitting in his favorite chair, his body rigid, only one hand in motion, he'd be absently stroking Bobby Lee sitting by his legs.

Frank was far away.

Sally's fierce love for her husband made her want to pierce his impenetrable wall at these times of withdrawal and help him fight his somber thoughts and any disquieting images. Over time, however, she realized that this was impossible. She was grateful that at least Bobby Lee was there to share these dark passages and be of some comfort.

Now in his eleventh year, Bobby Lee's health was declining rapidly. He ate little, slept more and walked slowly. He lost control of his bladder and was having accidents in the house, clearly embarrassed and contrite. Everyone was worried, and Sally watched anxiously as an enveloping stillness descended on Frank, performing all his expected daily rituals listlessly, mechanically.

When the bladder accidents increased, Frank lifted Bobby Lee into the cab of his truck and drove twenty-five miles to the nearest vet where blood was drawn for lab tests. The doctor, a gruff but cheerful man in his late fifties, ascribed the dog's decline to old age but could identify no specific problem.

Five days later, in the late afternoon, when the children and Frank's mother were off at a church bazaar, the vet called with the test results, and Sally, alone in the kitchen, had answered the phone.

"Sorry, Mrs. Butler," he said in a gravelly voice that somehow conveyed compassion. "It's complete renal failure. I'd advise bringing the dog in as soon as possible. Putting him down would be the best thing you could do for him at this point. He's suffering. It's quick and easy and painless."

Sally heard this death sentence as the world dropped away from her and she plunged into a dark void. "Thank you," was all she managed to mutter before putting the phone down. All she could think of was Frank. Her mind scrambled all her thoughts of how she should tell him. Unable to move, she started to weep. Deep, thunderous sheets of wailing, gurgling, moaning sounds rose up through her body, exploding in her throat as she shielded her mouth with her hands.

She didn't hear Frank's truck on the gravel driveway, and when he entered the kitchen and saw her tear-smeared face and bewildered eyes, he knew all. Silently, she rushed to him and buried her face in his neck. He pressed her to him and rhythmically they rocked back and forth in a macabre dance of consolation.

"How long?" he said finally.

She repeated everything the vet had said, almost word for word since his exact words were still etched sharply in her mind. She still clung tightly to him, and now she felt his body grow rigid. He released his hold on her and backed away, his face a mask of black resolve.

"No!" he said with a fierceness that frightened her. "No vet! I'll take care of this. It's my responsibility. I owe him that much."

In rapid motion, he left the kitchen and she heard him unlocking the hall closet where he kept his hunting rifle.

"Bobby Lee. Come!" he said quietly.

He walked back through the kitchen heading for the back door, carrying the rifle and a shovel. Bobby Lee limped slowly behind him, the dog's breath coming in short gasps, his tail down, his eyes following his master.

The back door closed, and Sally stood in the middle of the kitchen, transfixed by the onrushing events of the last few minutes. She turned her head to the kitchen window and watched Frank and Bobby Lee slowly disappearing into the darkening woods. Then a crushing thought flickered across her mind and she extended her arms toward their retreating figures as she half screamed, half wailed, "I never got to say goodbye!"

* * *

About two hundred yards into the woods was a small, rapidly flowing stream where Frank would often come with Bobby Lee when he was in one of his black moods. There was a tree trunk where he'd sit and gaze at the water gurgling against rocks and licking the embankment, and it always seemed to soothe him. Bobby Lee would sit, his shoulder touching Frank's leg, his ears alert, nostrils quivering, eyes scanning the near distance. On these outings Frank got in the habit of talking to Bobby Lee, sharing his feelings and dark memories of the war: the buddies he had lost; the carnage and destruction he had witnessed; the fear he had felt; the near loss of hope.

Bobby Lee would turn his head toward Frank, staring up at him with his big black eyes as though he was listening and understood. Frank found the visits to the stream and these private musings with his dog helped to relieve the stress and tension that built up inside him.

Now they came to the stream and Frank took his usual seat on the tree trunk. Bobby Lee, panting heavily, lay at his feet, too weak to stand or sit.

"I think this is the best place, don't you? We've had many peaceful times here together," Frank said. "It's our special place."

A brief wag of the tail was the dog's only response. His eyes, half closed, were still focused on Frank.

"I couldn't ask for a better friend," Frank said, scratching Bobby Lee's ruff and swallowing hard. "I'm so sorry," he said through clenched teeth. "I'm so sorry."

Bobby Lee's ears perked up. That mysterious channel of understanding that had always connected the man and his dog now seemed to take possession of Bobby Lee. Heaving a heavy sigh in what seemed like one long, last effort to respond to his master, Bobby Lee struggled to his feet and licked Frank's face. Frank looked directly into the dog's eyes and felt sure that he saw resolution and forgiveness. Then the dog fell on his side, panting heavily, his eyes closed.

"Thank you, buddy," Frank said, rising from his seat. "I know you know. It's time."

* * *

Sally stands at the kitchen window, clutching the edge of the sink, unable to move. She stares absently as the gathering gloom creeps across the grassy expanse of their back yard and is sucked into the deep forest void. She hears the gunshot and her body spasmodically jerks and then goes limp. She leans heavily against the sink to keep from falling.

Now, as the seconds pass, her mind registers the finality of that single shot, and she is already thinking of how she could effectively console her husband and break the news to the children, due back any minute with Frank's mother.

Sally walks across the kitchen toward the pantry but stops halfway, frozen in total confusion. There is no mistaking it. She has just heard another shot. She knows her husband to be a crack shot. Instant panic seizes her as the blackest thoughts flood her brain. **Oh, my god, NO! Not that!** She whips around to face the kitchen window, straining to see something, anything, but it's useless.

Frantically, she runs out the back door and blindly heads toward the woods, sobbing and gasping for breath. Her vision, clouded with tears, can't adjust to the oncoming night but she rushes on.

About fifty feet into the woods, she stumbles over a fallen branch and heavily hits the ground. She feels pain in her right shoulder but her terror drives her to ignore it and go on. She's struggling to stand when she feels an arm around her waist lifting her up. She smells him before she sees him: the familiar aromas of cigarettes, coffee and flannel. Giving vent to hysterical cries of relief she clutches Frank's shoulders in a fierce embrace.

"It's okay, honey. It's done," he says in a low, heavy voice. "I'll go back tomorrow when it's light and put a marker on the grave."

His words and the strength of his arms instantly sooth her as she tries to order her thoughts.

"But the second shot!" she says between deep gulps of air. The second shot. I thought..." She can't finish the sentence; can't say the thought out loud.

"After I dug the grave, I came up to get Bobby Lee and found a rattler next to him. I shot it," he says calmly. She nods, almost giddy from this explanation.

They cling to each other as they make their way quietly out of the black woods.

"You know, Sally, it was remarkable," Frank says as they reach the back yard and head for the house. "Bobby Lee really did understand. As least I felt that his last action was telling me it was okay. He was ready to go."

"I'm sure he did," she says, squeezing her husband's arm. "You two had such a bond, and Bobby Lee always understood a lot." Then she pauses before asking, "Who'll tell the children?"

"I will," he says decisively.

She smiles.

They walk together toward the welcoming lights of their family home.

Suppertime

"Our special report on the war in Afghanistan continues with live coverage by Chuck Miller in the Kandahar Valley.

"Mom, do we have to listen to this?" thirteen-year-old Karen Jameson wails as she sets the table for dinner in the family room where the fifty-five- inch flat-screen television shows a weary reporter in army fatigues, flak jacket and helmet.

"Yes, we do!" Liza Jameson replies emphatically to her daughter from the adjacent kitchen where she's mixing a large bowl of salad greens and Italian vinaigrette dressing. "It's important for us to stay abreast of what's happening in the world. How else can we have intelligent conversations about current events?"

This has been one of the bloodiest months in the longest war in American history, with more than forty American soldiers killed and many more wounded. The enemy seems to be growing stronger and more aggressive no matter how many planes and tanks and guns and soldiers we hurl at them. After ten long years,

Afghanistan defeated the Soviet Union, and now the outcome for the Unite States isn't looking any brighter.

"Karen, call your father and brother. Supper's ready."

While back home, in the halls of Congress and in coffee shops and homes across America—wherever people gather-- debate about the future course of this war rages, but here in the Kandahar Valley, soldiers are dying every day. There's no debate here about whether this war is right or wrong, winnable or impossible, or whether it should continue or end. Life for our soldiers is reduced to the simplest equation. Men and women know they have a job to do and any day they could be killed, so they do their job and try to stay alive. Not being constantly alert equals death. That's all that concerns them and all they focus on. But how long can the human mind and body bear the strain of being hyper-alert at all times? The answer seems to lie in the staggering statistics of soldier suicides, mental breakdowns and post-traumatic stress.

"Oh, boy! Veal Scaloppini and linguini!" fifteen-year-old Scott Jameson exclaims as he leaps into his seat at the family table.

"Did you wash your hands?" his mother asks sharply.

"Sure, Mom," Scott says, in that typical teenager's placating tone, reaching for the platter of veal.

"This looks great!" Frank Jameson says, coming in from the garage where he's been waxing his vintage sports car, in preparation for a car rally on Sunday. With a broad smile he surveys the dishes displayed on the table.

"After three nights of Chinese take-out and pizza, I thought we needed a decent, home-cooked dinner," Liza says in a mock-serious voice, carrying a pitcher of lemonade to the table. "I've been so busy soliciting donations for the club raffle that I've been neglecting my family."

As the death toll mounts, soldiers have no time to properly mourn their fallen comrades. As one soldier said to me, "We suck it up and go on doing our job." There's no sense of heroics here; just people doing their job. A dirty, gritty, sweaty, lethal job!

"Scottie, pass the linguini," Frank says.

"And take your elbows off the table," his mother adds.

But those statistics represent flesh-and-blood, young Americans who have made the greatest sacrifice for their country that anyone can make. And every day brings new casualties, new numbers. And the debates rage on. From Kandahar Valley this is Chuck Miller

"Mom, you're the only one interested in this stuff," Karen says, waving her fork at the television set. "Why can't we watch the reruns of *Happy Days*?"

"Because this is important," Liza replies. "Frank, did you remember to pick up the raffle tickets from the club?"

"I'm playing tennis with Billy Drake tomorrow after work so I'll pick them up then."

"Please don't forget. I promised Sally Young I'd take four books and I've got to get started selling them. I don't know why I let her talk me into taking so many books."

Lieutenant James Cartwell, thirty-two, from Roanoke, Virginia, killed by enemy fire...

"What's the big fund-raiser for this year?" Frank asks, pouring himself some lemonade.

'They want to resurface the tennis courts and reline the swimming pool." Liza says, helping herself to some salad. "At fifty bucks a chance, they could probably rebuild the club house, too."

"Not a bad idea," Frank says. "The men's locker room is pretty grungy."

"I hate the girls' locker room," Karen says, wrinkling her nose. "No privacy."

"And you don't want anyone to see how deformed you are," Scott says, smiling demonically at his sister.

"MOM!" Karen screams, as her cheeks grow hot and she glares at her odious brother.

"Stop that, both of you!" Liza says sternly.

While in the Senate, the Republicans are accusing the Democrats of being soft on defending their country by trying to cut off funding for the war in Afghanistan. But the Democrats respond that the war is bankrupting our country; there is no clear mission that can be successfully completed and more and more American soldiers are dying. And so the debate continues in the halls of Congress while outside, in the streets, a few people are parading in opposition to, or support of, this longest war in American history. But the demonstrations are nothing compared to those that took place all across the country towards the close of the Vietnam era, when young people were defiantly burning their draft cards and even World War Two veterans were voicing their opposition to the war. This is Peter Heath reporting from Washington.

Karen, you're not eating." Liza says, eyeing the meager portion of salad on her daughter's plate.

"Mom, you know I'm on a diet!" Karen wails. "Cheerleader tryouts are next week."

"You think you're going to get skinny in one week, Thunder Thighs?" Scott says, clearly finding this funny.

"Shut up, fungus breath!" his sister hotly replies.

"That's quite enough," Liza intervenes. "Karen, you've got to eat something besides a little salad. Have some veal."

"The sauce is fattening," Karen says.

"Then scrape it off," Frank suggests, "but you don't know what you're missing." Smiling at his wife, Frank says, "Honey, this is delicious!"

We want to give names and faces and a little history to those statistics that scrawl across our television screens every night. Let's start with a few of the soldiers who were killed last week. Corporal Dwayne Madison from Seluca, Kentucky was twenty-three when he was hit by an IED and killed instantly. He leaves a wife and two-year-old twins. His wife reports that he joined the Army after he had been laid off from his job in a bottling plant and couldn't find work.

'Dad, when is the new boat going to be delivered?" Scott asks.

"I called the Walker Boatyard today and Mr. Walker said we should have it by next weekend."

"Great! With those twin engines it should be awesome for water skiing!" Scott says enthusiastically. His father nods his agreement.

"But I liked our sailboat," Karen says.

"You can still sail the sunfish," Frank says cheerfully.

"That's so small, it's no fun," Karen says with a growing pout.

"Well, honey, when you grow up, you can buy your own sailboat, as big as you like," Frank says with mock seriousness. "How's that?"

Karen doesn't reply and her scowl deepens.

Private Jason Peters, eighteen, from Sonoma, California... killed when a rocket hit his Humvee. Jason's two sisters said that Jason loved surfing and racing his ATV. According to his platoon buddies, he was always ready with a joke and a prank. During boot camp, he had won a citation for marksmanship and was a crack shot.

"Let's take the new boat on a maiden voyage to Jenkers Island and have a nice picnic," Lisa suggests, catching some of Scott's enthusiasm. "We can invite Nolie and Gramps."

"Ah, Mom, they're no fun," Scott says, deflated. Nolie gets seasick and Gramps is always ordering us around.

Frank looks across the table to his wife and cocks an eyebrow. "I can see how well our children will look after us when we get to be my father's age."

Lisa smiles.

Staff Sergeant Eric Gomez from Boqueron, Puerto Rico was completing his third tour of duty, the first two having been in Iraq, when he was hit by a sniper's bullet. A career soldier, he leaves a wife and three children, ages five through eleven, and two stepchildren, fourteen and sixteen. Sergeant Gomez was thirty-two.

"Dad, Jake Mayer and his family just came back from Paradise Island and had a great time," Scott says. "Can we go there next winter?"

"I thought you wanted to go back to Cancun," Frank replies.

Scott shakes his head. "Cancun's okay but Jake says Paradise Island is awesome."

"What about our plan to ski in the Rockies this winter?" Lisa interjects.

"Why can't we do both?" Scott asks with a big smile.

""We'll see," is his father's noncommittal response.

Corporal Jose Espada, twenty-three, from Newark, New Jersey, killed by a rocket while sleeping in his tent. The father of one son, three, Corporal Espoda was on his second tour of duty and had been wounded while serving in Iraq but returned to duty. He had just become a citizen and, according to his wife, was very proud to be serving his adopted country.

"I want to go to Las Vegas," Karen announces, "and see all the fantastic hotels and the big shows. Roberta Stover went there with her parents last year and raved about it."

"Put it on your list for the future," Frank suggests.

"I never get to go where I want to go!" Karen moans.

"That's not true," Liza says evenly. We went to Disney World last year at your request."

"One time!" Karen says with a dramatic wave of her arms.

Staff Sergeant Clarence Brown, twenty-eight, killed by an IED, was a career soldier with ten years in the Army and leaves a wife and three children, ages five, seven and eight.

"Frank, how is your case coming?" Liza asks.

"Great!" Frank says, twirling the linguini around his fork. "My part is done. John Rodabuck is giving the summation tomorrow. We all feel confident that we're going to win. And that means big bucks for the firm."

"And you get a percentage of the settlement, right, Dad?" Scott says with sudden interest.

"Yes, Scottie, as a partner, I get a share of all the firm's revenues."

"So now, maybe we can move and get a bigger house? I'm sick of sharing a bathroom with Karen."

"You're not sharing a bathroom with your sister," Liza corrects him patiently. "It's a Jack and Jill arrangement, and you each have your own sink and john in a private compartment. You're only sharing the shower in the middle compartment."

"I hate sharing anything with **him**!" Karen announces.

"Anyway," Liza adds, ignoring her daughter's petulant remark, "this is a perfectly beautiful house and you should be grateful."

The sullen looks on her children's faces silently convey their response.

Corporal Kevin Masterson, twenty-one, from Seattle, Washington, was wounded by sniper fire while on patrol with his platoon and died two days later in a field hospital. Corporal Masterson and his fiancé were planning to be married as soon as he completed his tour of duty. He leaves behind a one-year-old daughter, and his fiancé is expecting their second child in four months.

"I want some more," Scott says.

"Please," his mother adds, handing a still-half-filled platter across the table.

"Please," Scott repeats offhandedly, grabbing the platter and filling his plate with veal and linguini.

"Frank, I have to take my car in for a tune-up tomorrow. And you know how long that takes, so I probably won't be able to pick Scott up after soccer practice or take Karen to dance class."

"You shouldn't take it to the dealer," Frank says gently. "They charge an arm and a leg and they're always slow."

"I know, but I feel more confident with them," Liza says.

"I've got that tennis game with Billy Drake tomorrow afternoon," Frank reminds her.

"I could skip dance class," Karen says brightly.

"No, you won't," Liza quickly responds

"Well, I can't skip soccer, Mom," Scott says assertively.

"Liza, Billy Drake has brought a lot of business to my firm. I just can't cancel on him at the last minute."

Liza pauses to think of a solution.

Corporal Masterson's mother, like so many mothers of fallen soldiers, exhibits her own form of bravery. We contacted her in her home in Seattle and she had this to say: My son Billy died for what he believed in. He loved his country and was willing to defend our freedoms against the Muslims who want to destroy us. I'm proud of what he accomplished and I'll honor his memory for the rest of my life. I'm only sorry his father isn't alive to see what a hero our son is. He was a war hero, too, in Kuwait. And his granddaddy was in Vietnam. We're a proud military family.

"Dad, how come you were never a soldier?" Karen suddenly asks her father.

"Because, honey, as Dick Cheney, said, 'I had other priorities.'"

Private Lamar Johnson, nineteen, from Asheville, North Carolina...

"I suppose I can call the dealer and see if they can take me on Saturday," Liza says. "But that means you'll have to take Scottie to his SAT Prep class, Frank. It's only an hour."

"What time is his class?" Frank asks.

"Nine," Scott answers, "but I don't mind missing it."

"Not at these prices, mister," his mother says emphatically.

"I can drop you off before my golf game." Frank says. We're scheduled to tee off at 9:30"

"And I'll call George's parents and you can get a ride home with them," Liza says, pleased with the solution to this minor scheduling problem.

"What about my karate class?" Scott says

"**That** I don't mind your missing one week," Liza replies.

"Ah, Mom!" Scott yells, clearly disappointed.

"We all have to make sacrifices," his mother says.

Private Jonathan Neilson, eighteen, had just arrived in Afghanistan two weeks before his vehicle hit a roadside bomb and he was killed. He had recently graduated from Washloo Regional High School in High Falls, Minnesota. Under his picture in his Year Book was written, Future Undecided, Probably the Army.

"Honey, where's the remote?" Frank asks. "I want to get the stock report."

"By the way, Mom, I think I lost my cell phone," Karen announces.

"What's for dessert?" Scott asks.

Lisa ignores the voices around her, temporarily preoccupied with her own concerns.

Private Taqisha Summers, twenty-one, from New Orleans, Louisiana, a single mother of two girls, one and two, left her children in the care of their grandmother and joined the Army after overcoming drug addiction. According to her mother, she loved being a soldier, loved the military discipline, and wrote home that the army had saved her life. She was killed when a series of explosions ripped through the convoy she was traveling in.

"Frank, I'm really worried about selling all those chances for the club fundraiser."

She gazes around the table. No one is listening.

The Defining Moment

"I've decided to join the army," Douglas said with a mixture of pride and hesitancy as he finished his breakfast the morning after his graduation from high school. He had been practicing this announcement for several days, the wording of it, the time and place, but haphazardly it had just come out, and now he felt relieved.

His mother was in the midst of wiping the kitchen counter and had her back to him when he made his announcement. He watched as her hand froze in place and her back stiffened, making her appear taller than she was.

He waited for some response. When none came, he added, "Me and Tommy and Ben talked it over and we're going in together."

Tommy and Ben were his two closest friends since the third grade, and their bond was indissoluble. They had never been good students, had never been much as athletes, and had never been particularly popular. But that didn't seem to matter because they had one another to share jokes, discuss girls, listen to music, play video games, dream about the future and while away weekends in the pleasure of this secret society of three.

The secure world of high school had finally ended. With little ambition, few job prospects and no thought of college, their decision seemed eminently practical. All three boys came from working class families with assorted relatives who had been in the military. Spurred by vague notions of earning respect for their patriotism, as well as meeting unforeseen challenges to prove their self-conscious, emerging manhood, the three boys had decided that today was the time for announcing their plans to their families.

Finally, without turning to face him, his mother spoke. Her voice sounded far off. "When did you decide this?"

"A couple months ago," Douglas responded, grateful to have made his announcement, thereby moving his plan one step closer to reality.

Now she turned and looked directly at him with a fierce look betraying the strong emotions welling up inside her.

"And you didn't think it was something to talk over with me before you decided?" she asked, her voice quivering slightly, her eyes already misting.

He knew this would be difficult for her and he hated to see her clear signs of distress. Since his father's sudden death when he was ten, they had been a tightly fused unit of two.

"Mom, I'm sorry. I had to make this decision on my own."

"With Tommy and Ben," she said quickly, anger seeping into her tone.

He avoided her intense stare and rose from the table. "It's just somethin' I have to do," he said, eager to end this scene.

"Why?" she asked, her voice louder now.

He struggled for an answer that might placate her, settling on a patriotic appeal.

"Dad and grandpa were soldiers. I want to be one, too."

"Wait, Douglas," she said as he headed out of the kitchen, and the urgency in her voice made him turn and face her.

"So you want to be a soldier like your father and grandfather," she said in a curious tone he could not decode but instantly put him on the defensive.

"What's wrong with that?" he asked, half defiantly.

She moved to the table and sat down.

"Please listen for a minute," she said, motioning to the chair he had just vacated. Reluctantly, he returned to it.

Her voice was softer now. "Do you remember what your father did in the army?"

"Sure," he said, feeling that talking about his father's active duty in Vietnam would refocus the conversation into more positive channels. "He was a medic."

Her lips formed a slight smile. "And do you know why he was a medic?"

Confusion swept across his face in response to this unexpected question. Pictures of his father in uniform, a young man not much older than he was now, were filed in a photograph album that he and his mother had, together, looked through many times in the months after his father's death from a sudden, massive heart attack. They both found consolation in this ritual of recalling memories suggested by the many pictures memorializing the stages of his father's life.

As a young boy Douglas was especially proud of his father's army pictures, but now he realized from his mother's question that he had scant knowledge of any details surrounding his father's military service.

Reading the uncertainty on her son's face, his mother said, "Your father was a pacifist."

Douglas had no clear definition of this word and stared blankly at his mother.

"When he was drafted to fight in Vietnam, your father refused to kill anybody and chose to be a medic because he didn't have to carry a gun."

Douglas digested this surprising information as his mother continued. "He served honorably until he was wounded and sent back home. You've seen his medals."

His father's medals were in a small leather box that his mother had allowed him to keep in his room. Douglas flashed back to when he was younger, after his father died, and how he would often open the box and play with them, pinning them on his shirt and looking at himself in the mirror, pretending to be a decorated hero. This act made him feel closer to his father. He felt proud that his father and his father's father had been decorated soldiers, and he hoped some day to follow in their footsteps.

"Do you know what made your father a pacifist?" his mother now asked, interrupting his memories. To this challenging question he had no hint of an answer, and his face registered a blank look.

"Your grandfather's experience in the Second World War," she said with a steely glint in her eyes. This last revelation plunged him into total confusion. He had never heard anything about his grandfather, who had died when he was two, except how bravely he had served in France.

As though she were reading his mind, his mother continued. "Your grandfather fought in the European war for more than a year before he had one experience that changed his life and he refused to kill any more Germans. Because he had fought so bravely up to that point, the army refused to court martial him and gave him a psychiatric discharge and sent him home. He came back a changed man.

Douglas listened attentively to his mother as a different, contradictory picture of his grandfather was now taking shape. He struggled to reconcile all this new information with the simple, distilled picture that had been handed down to him.

"Would you like to learn more about what changed your grandfather's attitude toward the war?" his mother asked gently.

When Douglas, still befuddled, answered "Yeah," his mother unexpectedly rose from the kitchen table and said, "Come with me."

Meekly he followed her up the stairs to the storage room on the second floor of their small house. She headed for a trunk in a corner and removed a box overflowing with old curtains from the top of the trunk as dust mites swirled around their heads. Opening the trunk, she rummaged through its contents until she found what she was looking for. She extracted a large tin box and from that she took a manila envelope marked "personal" and handed it to her son with a solemn air.

"Read this, Douglas, and maybe it will give you a better understanding of what being a soldier really means."

They left the storage room and Douglas, feeling anxious about what the contents of the envelope might reveal, retreated to his bedroom, and closed the door. He sat on his bed and opened the envelope. It contained several sheets of a handwritten letter. The ink had faded but the handwriting was clear, strong and precise. At the top of the first page he saw the date, February 8, 1944. Feeling as though he were traveling back in time, he read on.

My dearest wife,

I will try to explain what has recently happened to me and why I now feel so different about the war. All my life I have been surrounded by guns. My father was a great hunter. He gave me my own gun when I was eight. I loved going hunting with him. I grew up seeing Jimmy Cagney and Edward G. Robinson and Humphrey Bogart killing people and getting killed in the movies. I never thought anything about it. When I was drafted I didn't give it a second thought. I knew America had to fight the Germans and the Japs and I was happy to do my part. In all the battles and skirmishes I took part in, the enemy was usually at some distance and I was usually aiming at a group. I'd fire away and sometimes I'd see a German fall but I was never sure if it was my bullet or another soldier's bullet that killed him. It was like what I read once about firing squads. One gun has blanks and no one knows which gun it is, so each member of the squad can think there's a possibility that he didn't kill the person being executed.

About two weeks ago my battalion had just liberated another French town in the countryside after a three-day battle. Most of the men had gone ahead in pursuit of the retreating Germans. My platoon was assigned to do one last sweep of the town before pulling out. My buddies had fanned out across the town square and were searching all the buildings looking for any Germans that might be hiding. I entered the church with my rifle at the ready. The church had been badly damaged by our bombs so I made my way carefully through the rubble. I stepped into a small side chapel and that's where I saw the body of a German soldier. He was on the floor with his back propped up against the altar. His head was down on his chest and his right hand still held a revolver. His helmet was off and I saw some blood on his blond hair. I saw no signs of breathing and thought he was dead. Still I cautiously moved closer to him to check him out.

I was no more than three or four feet away when suddenly he lifted his head and looked directly at me. We were both startled and stared at each other in surprise. I froze and we stayed locked in our positions for only a few seconds but they seemed like hours. What I remember most about those seconds was his startling blue eyes. He looked like he was about seventeen, just a kid. Then it hit me that he looked a lot like John Hansen, my best friend in high school.

I thought about taking him prisoner but in the next split second I could see that wasn't possible. His eyes widened and I knew that we were facing a kill or be killed situation. Everything now seemed to take place in slow motion. I saw his right arm move and his hand holding the gun started to lift off the floor. My reflexes were faster. I raised my rifle and fired point blank at his chest. His body jerked once and then his hand with the gun fell limply back to the floor. His chest seemed to collapse as I heard a long, low whistling sound of air escaping from his body.

When people die in the movies, their eyes close. His didn't. His blue eyes kept staring at me as blood spread across the jacket of his uniform. The more I stared at him, the more he looked like John Hansen. Then I had the strangest thought. Did he have a high school buddy who looked like me? Did he notice the resemblance in those last few seconds? Did that thought distract him for one brief moment that gave me the advantage and resulted in his death? I couldn't get that stupid thought out of my head. I can still see his eyes with their look of surprise and something else. Was it momentary indecision? I checked his pulse and then I closed his blue eyes. In death his face had the appearance of a boy, not a man. I walked out of the cold shadows of the church into the bright sunshine and I knew I would never fire a gun again.

Anna, I can't explain it any other way. In my mind now every German looked like that blond kid, like someone I grew up with. I'm being held in isolation after I told my lieutenant that I wouldn't fight any more. The army is figuring out what to do with me. Officers keep visiting me and talking to me about duty, honor, battle fatigue and bad decisions. They mention the medals and commendations I've received. I listen but I can't get that German kid's face out of my mind. He haunts me.

I don't know what will happen next or when I'll see you. I know that what I've shared with you might be hard to understand but, dearest Anna, you've always had an understanding heart. This incident made the war so personal for me and made me see it in an entirely different light. I'll let you know what happens next.

Your loving husband,
Robert

Douglas lay back on his bed, motionless, thinking about his grandfather's experience. So much about his father and grandfather had been revealed to him today, it was difficult to take it all in. He thought long and hard about his grandfather's description of killing another person and asked himself how he might react in a similar situation. He couldn't come up with a satisfactory answer because the heroes in his video games kept popping into his head. As the minutes ticked by, his youthful optimism, his sketchily formed sense of patriotic duty, the lure of adventure and his loyalty to his two buddies helped him relegate nagging doubts to the back of his mind. Leaping from his bed, he bounded down the stairs, prepared to resist his mother's entreaties and eager to take on the world.

A Matter of Choice

By the year 2025, the wars in Iraq and Afghanistan had been raging for decades—so long that young people had never known a time of peace.

President Mitt Romney in 2012, President Scott Brown in 2016, President Patrick Kennedy in 2020 and now President George Prescott Bush, son of the former Governor Jeb Bush, in 2024, had all run successful campaigns promising secret plans to end the wars and bring our troops home.

But the Shiites and the Sunnis in Iraq continued their ferocious battles and the Kurds were now demanding an independent state. Each time the American troop strength dipped below a certain number, fierce fighting and human devastation raged across the landscape and American casualties rose. Each president, in turn, felt obliged to reinforce troop levels to restore a semblance of peace over the simmering hostilities. And so the Iraq war dragged on because no president, after all the human and financial resources that had been wasted on this war effort, wanted to abjectly admit defeat.

In Afghanistan, the porous border between that country and Pakistan allowed the enemy to disappear like fog, only to come roaring back when American redoubts were abandoned and troops withdrawn. The atrocities then committed against those Afghanis who were viewed as siding with the American forces became international headlines, compelling the current president, castigated roundly for lack of humanitarian compassion by the opposing party, as well as for not supporting our brave men and women fighting for our freedom, to renege on campaign pledges and send more troops.

Several minor terrorist attacks in Philadelphia, Seattle, San Diego and Washington D.C., plotted and executed by people living in America, resulted in virulent anti-Muslim protests, repeated violent clashes and strident calls for ejecting all Muslims from the country or internment similar to what we did with the Japanese in WW II.

Iran, Syria and Saudi Arabia all possessed nuclear weapons by this time, rendering the entire Middle East a powder key of conflicting interests, shifting alliances and warring sects, with China, the most powerful economy in the new decade, backing all agencies hostile to the United States.

Thus, a total withdrawal from Afghanistan was unthinkable, no matter how unpopular this war—and the war in Iraq—had become with the weary, inflamed public. Yet even back home, opinion was clearly divided.

The liberal wing of the Democratic Party stormed for immediate peace with huge rallies and demonstrations reminiscent of the Vietnam era. The Tea Baggers, who had started up after the election of President Obama, had taken over the Republican Party, eliminating all moderates, and, together with the neo-cons, were rampaging for annihilating all those countries that harbored or supported terrorists, including the use of nuclear arms. "Rub The Bastards Out" and "Nuke 'em To Hell" were popular bumper stickers prominently adorning pick-up trucks and SUVs around the country

As civil strife and disobedience mounted in clashes between left and right, conservative radio commentators—Glen Beck had been sidelined with an harassment charge by a member of his staff and the apoplectic Rush Limbaugh had suffered a massive stroke, but Sean Hannity was still on the air—shrilly fulminated that it was time for a full, final revolution in this country. They clamored for the establishment once again of a god-fearing, Christian nation that aggressively defended all its interests across the globe and that obliterated dissent by pinko- socialists, pansy peacemakers and bleeding-heart liberals who, it was asserted, were mostly atheists and not "real" Americans.

In the U.S. Senate, a war of words reached a fever pitch as Republican Senators from the South, Midwest and Western states excoriated their Democratic colleagues for being soft on terrorists, lacking patriotism and not having the backbone to bring the two wars to a victorious conclusion **by any means**.

For their part, the Democrats from the Northeast and West Coast states fulminated against the heartless, soulless bellicosity of their Republican confreres and said that the American people were bone weary of these interminable wars and only when peace was restored could America regain its economic world hegemony.

Accusations and *ad hominem* insults flew back and forth as frustration levels mounted over the static condition of affairs. No measure or bill presented in the Senate could find a simple majority willing to compromise, so the vituperative speeches and inexhaustible posturing, like the wars, dragged endlessly on. The whole country and its government seemed paralyzed by opposing views and indecisive actions.

Throughout the decades of these conflicts, the government, whether controlled by Republicans or Democrats, had waged war with only a volunteer army. As casualties increased, so, too, did the bonuses and pay scales offered to young men and women who enlisted in any branch of the armed forces. Bonuses for re-enlisting ballooned to impressive figures until our military cadres became mostly an elite, mercenary band.

With the longest period of economic stagnation in American history, not helped by the constant flip-flopping of the parties in power and their diametrically oppositional actions to revive the economy, more and more of the GNP was consumed by our war efforts as social services and infrastructure allocations shrunk and the national debt continued to rise.

Current polls revealed that nearly ninety percent of Americans felt that (1) the country was heading in the wrong direction, (2) things would not be getting better in the near future, and (3) their children would have a harder life than they did. Six months after each new president was elected, his or her support dropped to below twenty-five percent, while confidence in the government plummeted to all-time lows.

A young senator from Ohio, who had served with distinction in Iraq fifteen years earlier, wrote an op-ed piece for the New York Times titled Another Modest Proposal. The persuasive theme was that we should reintroduce the draft but this time military service of two years would be compulsory for all young men AND women with no exception except severe medical conditions. The conclusion of the article was compelling.

"It is time," wrote the senator, "that we return to more democratic ideals that have been the soul of our country, the engine of our progress and the beacon to the world. It is time we stopped waving the flag as a small minority of citizens march off to fight and die while the rest of us remain safely at home. If these wars, or any wars, are worth fighting, then we should all be committed to them, as we were in WW II. It is time that the leaders of our government, through their sons and daughters, have a direct stake in fostering, declaring, maintaining and prolonging wars. For too long we have sat comfortably on the sidelines, catching glimpses of war on television in an abstract, detached manner, through a medium associated more with entertainment than with reality. For too long the costs of war in both material and human terms have been delivered to us as impersonal, inert statistics. For too long we have dithered, squabbled, vacillated, temporized and procrastinated. It is time for true patriotism, not in words, hymns or songs but in deeds and actions, resolve and sacrifice, to again infuse our national purpose and revitalize the pride of our democratic citizenry. It is time for Americans to remember that throughout our history, including our stand against British tyranny before our country was even formed, we have risen to face, resolutely and resourcefully, any challenge to our rights and freedoms and our pursuit of happiness. It is time, America, for a dramatic move. It is time to act."

The country was in such a desperate mood that the senator's idea, couched in flamboyantly stirring rhetorical flourishes, struck a respondent chord in the collective consciousness. The op-ed piece was reprinted in newspapers across the country, featured on television news programs and the Ohio senator's website received over twenty million hits.

To the astonishment of many political pundits, this revolutionary idea caught fire and gained support from both the left and the right. Soon evangelical and mainline ministers were quoting esoteric Bible passages in announcing God's support of a universal conscription, while liberals embraced it as the fairest possible approach, regardless of class, status, wealth or influence. Even the conservative radio commentators came on board, bloviating about honor, duty and country, and recognizing the strong appeal these notions had for their macho audience.

Conservatives pictured a huge expansion of the armed forces that could quickly overwhelm any enemy in Iraq and Afghanistan and anywhere else where America's preeminence was challenged. Liberals saw it as a further guarantee of peace and greater protection for the little countries against big, neighboring bullies. Corporations envisioned a huge expansion of all supplies connected with soldiering, from armaments and guns to clothing and condoms. Feminists embraced it, reluctantly, as a necessary step toward full equality with men.

In a matter of months, the groundswell of feverish support for this action from across the country and every spectrum of the political field reached an overwhelming crescendo that swept away any timorous voices of opposition. The young Senator from Ohio, who had won election as an independent, was now being touted as the next presidential candidate by both Republicans and Democrats.

Mindful of his low approval ratings, President George Prescott Bush quickly became an ardent supporter. The members of Congress, besieged by emails, text messages, calls and visits from members of their constituency, fell into line. In the House, with only seven dissenting votes—all from House members who were retiring at the end of their current terms—the bill for universal conscription was quickly passed.

In its procrustean fashion, the Senate took up the bill at a more leisurely pace, as individual senators took the opportunity to quote Greek philosophers or, in other pompous ways, to try to briefly gain the public's attention, thereby burnishing their own image. Once the grandstanding had run its course, the bill was passed 94 to 4, and universal conscription was implemented six months after that.

Beneath all this patriotic fervor and swaggering posturing there was great unease across that level of society that was used to influencing and making laws which mostly served them favorably. Wives of senators and congressmen who had sons and daughters or grandchildren of conscription age railed against their husbands for jeopardizing their progeny's safety, but the politicians chose political survival over family security. Now, however, the two wars were seen through an entirely different lens. Once the first wave of enthusiasm had crested, reality swept in.

For the first time in America's history, women, who had fought long and hard for equal rights, now found themselves—if of a certain age—equally obliged to give two years of military service to their country; whether in combat or support services was their one option. Mothers of children under ten were excluded and the birthrate in America rose dramatically.

The sons of wealth had escaped wars through college deferments—no longer given—or, during the Vietnam era, by escaping to foreign countries. But in the present charged atmosphere such an action would bring disgrace upon the family and possibly condemn the escapee to lifelong exile.

All medical deferments were zealously scrutinized by a national review board, and the punishment for malingering was not only social opprobrium but could include incarceration. The American Psychiatric Association was overwhelmed with reports from psychiatrists that they could not handle the increased number of young patients having nervous breakdowns or claiming to have strange mental disorders.

The rich and powerful now found themselves reduced to the status of any ordinary citizen when it came to surrendering their young family members to the maw of the draft. No longer was it primarily the young black, Latino and fervently patriotic men from impoverished backgrounds with little formal education who willingly heard the call to duty as an escape from dead-end jobs and limited futures. Now the scions of wealth and privilege were confronting the prospect of sacrificing comfort, security and possibly even brilliant futures for a rigorous, menial military regimen including the risk of maiming or death.

A private hue and cry convulsed homes, townhouses and estates across America and immediately influenced further decisions regarding the two wars.

The conservatives who for many years had advocated the application of nuclear weapons to all enemies, actual or suspected, soon came to understand that with the rapid proliferation of nuclear arsenals among small countries, the chances of successful retaliation against our cities and towns increased exponentially. This left only massive conventional forces as a means of achieving victory. Even among the most jingoistic patriots, fissures of concern soon arose over the ultimate sacrifice of children to the prolonged pursuit of a vindicating end to the wars.

The liberals, who for over a decade had demanded an immediate cessation of hostilities, now revolted at the prospect of losing their loved ones in fruitless battles and renewed their call for peace.

The two wars were no longer seen in disembodied terms of troop surges and casualty statistics mentioned briefly in newspapers and on television. Pro-war sloganeering phrases, such as balance of power, stopping terrorists, fighting for freedom and protecting our democratic way of life, suddenly seemed hollow.

Now these far-off wars were real, up-close and personal, palpably affecting all households, not just a few. Even the elderly with beloved grandchildren of draft age were directly involved and ferociously protective of their stake in perpetuating their line through succeeding generations.

The debates and speeches in Congress took on new tones, new perspectives, as senators and congressmen applied their powers of persuasion and oratorical skills to convincing both themselves and the public, through tortured reasoning, vaulted rhetoric and ponderous circumlocution, that an imminent withdrawal of all combat troops from both Afghanistan and Iraq would result in a great victory. The exhausted and anxious public eagerly supported this charade. Within months, amidst flurries and fanfares of self-congratulations, America's foreign wars had come to a jubilant, if dubious, conclusion.

Extremist Muslim groups could no longer recruit young men and women with the threat of America's encroachment on Muslim territory and ideals. While internal struggles persisted in both Iraq and Afghanistan, overt hostilities toward America gradually abated, especially when the only American forces left in those countries were building schools, hospitals and housing for the people.

Oh, yes, the young senator from Ohio ran for president under the banner of a newly formed Peace With Dignity Party and won by a landslide, becoming the first female president of The United States. Universal conscription for any armed engagement with another country remained the law of the land, and America enjoyed an enduring era of peace and prosperity, promoting its democratic ideals by example rather than force.

The Dead of Night

    The huge cargo plane, like some giant prehistoric bird, swoops down out of the deep night sky, taxies slowly across the tarmac and comes to a lumbering halt. I stand behind the chain-link fence with a small cluster of people and already an electric current is racing through me.

    I watch in a tense silence, motionless, as the belly of the plane slowly opens and descends to the ground. My eyes sweep up the ramp as cold fluorescent lights flick on in the plane's interior. I hear sharp intakes of breath and audible gasps as the people around me catch their first glimpse of the coffins.

    A woman standing a few feet away from me begins to sob, leaning into a man who has his arm around her and is gently patting her shoulder. A tall, brawny man standing at my side mutters "Jesus Christ" and then falls into silence. There are no children in the crowd.

    A military guard of seven men who have been standing at attention near the plane now slowly, with a precise, exaggerated cadence, ascend the ramp and surround the coffin nearest to our view. With one graceful motion they lift it and, led by a soldier in front with his sword raised in a salute, they descend the ramp in gliding, almost balletic strides. Edges of the American flag draping the coffin flutter slightly, catching the soft breeze kissing the night. Another line of five soldiers standing at attention offer a prolonged salute as the coffin is carried past them.

I watch this hypnotically choreographed scene with bitterness and despair so deep that I think at any moment I might leap with a Herculean effort over the fence and hurl myself at anyone in my path, mindlessly striking out in my red-hot rage. My hands are trembling and I can feel trickles of sweat at my temples and down my sides, although it's a cool night.

I count sixteen coffins in all. Each coffin is carried ceremoniously into a hanger and laid in a neat row. I do not know which coffin is my son's.

The men lining the fence are standing at attention, hands over hearts. More women are now weeping. I neither salute nor weep. My mouth is bone dry and my temples are pounding out a rat-tat-tat drumbeat of pain.

I turn to look at the faces surrounding me, mostly black and brown, and see frozen masks of deepest grief. I search each face for any sign of my shared rage but find none, which only increases my blazing indignation. I want to disrupt, to smash this staged Kabuki-like facade of honor and reverence that hides the callous indifference to the expendable lives of the unimportant. I want to scream at this mournful crowd, "Is this a hero's welcome--carried home in the dead of night, with no reporters or photographers allowed so that the public can be spared the realities of this mindless war? Do you now realize—has it sunk in yet—what you and your loved one have been asked to give?"

Tomorrow, television news programs will have some telegenic young reporter momentarily lowering his or her voice slightly to casually announce the war dead for the day, the week or the month, and then pausing for a second—a mere heartbeat—before flashing a broad smile and turning to sports scores or the latest celebrity or political scandal that is the heart of the media's bloodstream. These statistics will be received by the American public, sitting comfortably around their big-screen television sets, with not even a flicker of recognition, not even a pause in their eating whatever meal or snack is part of their viewing ritual, so anesthetized have we become to the carnage—the spilling of blood and guts, the maiming, the excruciating agonies-- that's part of any war.

Each one of these flat, easily forgotten numbers of the dead was a living, breathing, dreaming, aspiring young man or woman who was a son, daughter, spouse, parent, grandchild, niece or nephew in some family. And that family now, like me, feels the full weight, the crushing awareness that this unique, beloved person has been stripped of individuality, humanity, life itself, and is now a mere statistic, like how many people ran in the Boston marathon or how many medals the U.S.A. won in the latest Olympics. Just numbers endlessly spewed out from the maw of the insatiable media, numbing the public into dull resignation and forgetfulness.

Only to us, the people behind this chain-link fence, does the person in each of those coffins matter. Only we must forever feel this loss and be haunted with the memories of who they were and who they hoped to become. Only we must grapple with the biggest, hardest question of all: Why did they die? For what commanding reason, what noble cause, what lofty principal did they offer their lives in sacrifice? Or, more pointedly, did their government, their leaders, willingly and without justification sacrifice them?

Have some of the people surrounding me here already settled on their answers, entombing their grief with the simple, confirmed conviction that their loved ones died in defense of their country, their freedom, our way of life, or in fitting retribution for 9/11? How fortunate you are! How I envy you. How many gathered here are like me, with no answers, only doubts and confusion and rage?

When my grandfather fought in the First World War and then my father fought in WW II, it seemed much simpler. The enemy was a clear and distinct aggressor that had to be defeated. After that, our wars became murkier, less penetrable for root causes that any average American could easily understand as clear and present danger. Yes, we wanted to stop Communism, that great bug-bear that, according to our political voices, menaced us from every side.

Until the Vietnam War turned into a ferocious cycle of befuddling deaths, hitting the mainstream because of the draft, we pretty much went along with what our leaders preached—the religion of war in the name of peace. Secure in my college deferment, I joined my fellow students in marches and rallies protesting the war. We could afford to burn our draft cards because our status as students kept us safe. Our youthful zeal was laudable but, still, we knew that no true test of courage and sacrifice awaited us. That was for others.

Then came 9/11 and Iraq.

I'm just an average guy, a high school music teacher who coached my son's Little League baseball team. I get up every day, go to work, worry about keeping my job, about how long my car will last, about paying my bills, about helping my kids get a start in life. I grapple with the rising cost of everything from groceries and mulch to home insurance and dental care, and struggle to save. Before my wife died two years ago, I helped her clean up after dinner and I helped my kids with homework and helped my neighbors in emergencies. Then I added chief cook and bottle washer to my list of duties. The home that I own, along with the bank that holds a big mortgage, always needs repairs or broken appliances to be replaced. I never seemed to have the time or the inclination or the energy to pay too much attention to what was happening in the wide world until something knocked on my door and turned my life upside down.

That's the way it was for me with Iraq. One minute the whole country was in a suspended state of disbelief, still suffering from the shock of the 9/11 attack and vowing to get the terrorists who did this heinous act; the next minute the Bush-Cheney team was banging the war drums and declaring an all-out war against Iraq's Saddam Hussein. For me, that's when the shit really hit the fan.

No matter how much I tried to settle in my own mind a justifiable reason for sending our kids over to Iraq, I couldn't come up with a satisfactory answer. Charges that Iraq possessed weapons of mass destruction were soon disproved. Charges of Iraq's direct involvement in 9/11: disproved. Charges that Al Qaeda had been sheltered in Iraq: disproved.

Then I started to hear our leaders say that our real goal was to establish a functioning democracy in the Middle East. But that was countered with mini-history lessons on TV and radio about the thousand-year Sunni-Shia battles and how Iraq, except when under the brutal thumb of tyrants, had never functioned as a unified country with a central authority. No loyalty or personal identity extended beyond family, tribe and religious sect.

Whatever the shifting arguments for war, which I began to think were as changeable as the shifting sands of the Iraqi desert, the politicians were always talking about 9/11 and patriotism, wearing the lapel-pin flag and pounding into the public that this was a righteous cause.

I could have remained confused in a remote, vaguely mistrustful way if my son Craig hadn't decided to join the Marines with two of his buddies after graduating from high school. That's when the war came home and stood nose to nose in front of me, no longer abstract, now powerfully personal and in my face. Nothing I said could talk Craig out of his decision. He saw this challenge as a great adventure, a test of his young manhood, a call to arms following in the tradition of his forebears, if not his father. I even harbored a nagging fear that he was secretly ashamed of me and wanted to restore the family's honor with his service to the country.

From the time Craig arrived in Iraq, my life took on a heightened intensity, a sharp-edged scrutiny of each day's war news, each new political rationale for placing my son in harm's way and ultimately claiming his life.

I'm grateful that his mother isn't alive to bear this cross but, for selfish reasons, I'm sorry that I can't share my grief with her.

So now my son and the sons and daughters in those other fifteen coffins will come home one last time and there will be one, quiet moment when the world acknowledges their sacrifice, as a soldier hands a grieving parent or spouse the ceremoniously folded flag that now drapes their coffins in this cold, impersonal, metal hanger. I have been to the funerals of other soldiers and heard the prepared speech about a nation grateful for their sacrifice. And I suppose that at some distant time in the future there will be a war memorial for this war, with lofty sentiments about honor and duty inscribed in cold stone. Or, maybe like the Vietnam Memorial, each of the names of the war dead will be chiseled in granite, as a permanent testimony to what they gave for their country.

But I'll tell you the hard truth. No words, no speeches, no gestures can take away the raw, gut-deep anger I feel for suspecting that my son's life was discarded by uncaring old men who wage wars for political or economic or ideological calculations and, with sublime indifference, ignore the costs to others.

When Dick Cheney, an outspoken architect of this war, was asked by a reporter why he hadn't served his country as a young man during the Vietnam era, he disdainfully replied, "I had other priorities." That scornfully arrogant statement echoes endlessly through my head as I watch these coffins being unloaded, and I think of the other priorities, besides serving their country, that these young men and women most assuredly had for the future that will never be fulfilled.

It is true, what someone once observed, that old men wage wars that young men fight. To that statement, those of us gathered here at Andrews Air Force Base, must add, "And die for." The immediate follow-up question has to be, "And for what?" This is the burning question that rages in my brain: What did my son die for? Was it for the uninterrupted flow of oil? The unimpeded growth of multi-national corporations? The rich to get richer? The egotistical whimsy of the powerful? Every day on television news channels, I see these questions being debated by political opponents, but for me, and these other families here tonight, this is no longer a probing intellectual exercise but a matter targeting life and death.

These questions bring me to the edge of a steep, dark precipice, for if, in my heart, the definitive answer to any of them is yes, then my ongoing torture must be that my son died for nothing that I recognize as noble or transcendent or worthy of a moral democracy.

The dead soldiers gathered here are now at peace but we, the living, must find a separate peace. I think of Lincoln's humble words, "The world will little note nor long remember what we say here." He was wrong, but, sadly, his words are true for these men and women who now slide beneath the slipstream of history, joining countless, anonymous foot soldiers serving the ambitions and egos of other, more exalted figures in history's current.

Tomorrow there will be more statistics, more cargo planes emptying their sacred freight, more relatives replacing me at this very gate, speechlessly gazing at the secret ritual conducted under cloak of darkness, keeping vigil, bearing heartbreaking witness to the costs of war. We, alone, who loved them, are left to mourn for them, to remember, to cherish, to reconcile in our own hearts the meaning of their sacrifice. Perhaps, like me, for some of these families that reconciliation will be unendurably long and painfully frustrating.

I stand in the shadows of this warm, spring night and notice with a fleeting sense of irony how the plane hanger's harsh lights accentuate the vivid red, white and blue of the flags draping the coffins--such bright colors suggesting the upbeat, hopeful nature of our country and its people! Yet beneath each flag lies the mute, stark testament to our country's dark side and the terrible, unsatisfactory price that some of us must pay for maintaining the illusion of righteous wars and noble intentions.

For me, it's too high a price to pay. I want my son back! Goddammit! I want my son back!